THE AWARD

The Award

by Lydie Salvayre
translated by Jane Davey

Four Walls Eight Windows
New York

© English translation 1997 Four Walls Eight Windows, Inc.
Originally published as *La Médaille*, © 1993 Editions du Seuil.

Published in the United States by
Four Walls Eight Windows
39 West 14th Street, room 503
New York, N.Y., 10011

First printing August 1997.

All rights reserved. No part of this book may be reproduced, stored in a data base or other retrieval system, or transmitted in any form, by any means, including mechanical, electronic, photocopying, recording, or otherwise, without the prior written permission of the publisher.

Library of Congress Cataloging-in-Publication Data:
Salvayre, Lydie.
[Médaille. English]
The award / by Lydie Salvayre; translated by Jane Davey.
p. cm.
ISBN 1-56858-075-4
I. Davey, Jane. II. Title.
PQ2679.A52435M4313   1997
843'.914—dc20   96-23708
    CIP

10 9 8 7 6 5 4 3 2 1

Printed in the United States

To Elizabeth,
to Bernard.

"While grace is being said after meat, do you and your brethren take the chairs from behind the company, so that when they go to sit again they may fall backwards, which will make all merry; but be you so discreet as to hold your laughter till you get to the kitchen . . ."

Jonathan Swift,
Directions to Servants

FIRST SPEECH	I
MEDAL RECIPIENT'S RESPONSE	II
SECOND SPEECH	23
MEDAL RECIPIENT'S RESPONSE	33
THIRD SPEECH	47
RESPONSE OF THE MEDAL RECIPIENT'S WIDOW	59
FOURTH SPEECH	69
MEDAL RECIPIENT'S RESPONSE	81
FIFTH SPEECH	89
MEDAL RECIPIENT'S RESPONSE	101
SIXTH SPEECH	109
MEDAL RECIPIENT'S RESPONSE	121
SEVENTH SPEECH	125
MEDAL RECIPIENT'S RESPONSE	139
FINAL SPEECH	147

FIRST SPEECH

Dear friends.

You have successfully met our criteria for selection. Your conformity is perfect. Your conduct is exemplary. Your level of endurance is superior to the national average. We need no more proof of your dedication. Day after day, your performances continue to dazzle us. Ladies and Gentlemen, Bravo!

On the occasion of this traditional ceremony, we are pleased to introduce our plan for social regeneration, conceived as a reward for your merits.

First of all, we studied the question of your accommodations. The old system of dormitories seemed obsolete to us. We have developed a taste for innovation. Individual rooms were the unanimous choice. Transparent ones, if you please.

A ROOM FOR EVERYONE!

From now on, each of our bachelors will have the pleasure of a room to himself! A residence with eight hundred units has just been constructed. Each room has a floor area of six square meters and all modern conveniences. They are climate-controlled. The air is filtered. No need to open the windows. The furniture, secured to the floor so it cannot be removed, was designed by a renowned interior decorator.

We have relaxed internal regulations. We will not back away from moral progress. From this day onwards, all types of visits will be permitted, including those of young women. Visitors will be allowed into the rooms, once they have revealed their identities to the supervisor. Dogs are not allowed. All unauthorized persons will be immediately expelled. We are vigilant where your safety is concerned.

Needless to say, our views on sexuality have evolved considerably. As a matter of fact, we contend that they have changed completely. The days of bromide insidiously slipped into your café au lait are dead and gone. We no longer condemn onanism. Quite the contrary. Concerning the sexual government of our workers, we are all in favor of joint worker-management control. We are openminded. We particularly advocate masturbation for those of you not wise enough to equip yourself with a spouse.

Let us be blunt about this. Masturbation can be performed either at home or during breaks. Pull your foreskin upwards, then downwards, like a piston. Repeat this movement from twenty to fifty times, according to need, while steadily increasing your speed. Spurt. Next, wipe yourself off with a Kleenex, provided for your convenience in our latrines. We have anticipated your every necessity. Pull your pants back up and return to your place on the production line. You will get back to work with twice the enthusiasm.

We have paid equal attention to the question of your break. The decision has been made. Your break has been lengthened! We certainly don't lack audacity. It has been extended to fifteen minutes. Two fifteen-minute breaks a day, allowing you ample time to indulge in your favorite little pastimes.

FIFTEEN MINUTE BREAKS!

Gentlemen, we know how to systematize! Nothing is left to chance. We have analyzed your break period and broken it down into the following components :

- One minute for urination, allowing for the fact that in the ner-

The Award

vous and impulsive subject, the act is a series of brief stops and starts while in the lymphatic subject, it is a long, majestic and solitary process. Permit me a remark concerning this matter. Certain individuals, in an effort to avoid any drop in their production, are relieving themselves surreptitiously behind the machines. This conduct is repulsive and annoying to our engineers, who, judging by the violence of their reactions, seem to be endowed with olfactory instruments more sensitive than your own. Gentlemen, a bit of consideration, please! You're not dogs!

- Three minutes for defecation. We cannot over-stress the importance of performing this function outside the factory for reasons that would be unbecoming to broach before such a distinguished gathering. A little effort of the imagination should tell you why.
- And five minutes for food intake, based on thirty-two mastications per minute. Our experts cannot be faulted for lack of generosity.

That leaves you with six minutes to squander as you please. We respect everyone's freedom of choice. We wouldn't have it any other way.

Inside sources have reported that two of our workers, present here today, have been refusing their breaks in order to increase their quotas. Gentlemen, do not try to gain your foreman's notice. That's being overzealous. You are not here to get ahead. A true worker is a modest one. Get this through your skulls.

A TRUE WORKER IS A MODEST ONE

Let us proceed, if you don't mind, to more serious matters. A self-improvement program that we are continually refining will soon be made available to you. We have high hopes for our self-improvement program. We believe a perfected worker can double, triple, even quadruple his energy and compete with the best machines conceived by modern science. Fine tuning, adequate handling, a few words of encouragement or a good smack, figuratively speaking of course, and our newly galvanized worker will be unleashed. We look forward to the day when you will be fully energized and capable of slogging away without respite. This level of perfection, ladies and gentlemen, is our dream and goal. We make no attempt to conceal this from you.

Theories regarding fatigue and sleep requirements are unfortunately contradictory. Certain nitpickers estimate that rest is necessary for both body and soul. Others deem it superfluous and even consider it a vice. With our present knowledge, we are not in a position to make scientific pronouncements relative to this thorny question. But we do have our convictions. As far as I am concerned, rest is not only useless, it's unhealthy! Who needs it? Only lazy layabouts, that's who! What is it good for? Nothing! Because fatigue, gentlemen, is purely imaginary, a pretext for idleness, vain reveries, an odious alibi for shirking Duty which is Everything. Fatigue, therefore, must be eradicated. Without mercy!

FATIGUE IS NONEXISTENT

Ladies, gentlemen, fatigue is nonexistent. Fatigue is only the morbid product of dispirited souls, or should I say, souls corrupted by extremist propaganda. We must impress this upon you. We haven't given up hope that, one day soon, we will witness you working without interruption. In a sort of perpetual motion. Like flies. Perhaps this isn't the best example.

To help you ward off the illusion of exhaustion that can sometimes assail you, we recommend, once your work day is

The Award

over, that you begin another. Many of the most civilized countries, like Italy, Japan and Hungary, have adopted this progressive approach. Let us follow their example.

If you find yourself with any surplus energy, work in your vegetable patch when you get home. Your sleep, albeit brief, will be more sound.

Let us go back to our self-improvement program.

There will be a compulsory reassessment every four months. This will involve an endurance test on a stationary bicycle, an overhaul of the various systems, and a cardiac check.

You say, gentlemen, that your energy is depleted? Regain some of that youthful vitality by visiting our consulting physician. Do you balk at a job? Are your organs defective? Do your limbs rebel or become overtly hostile when effort is required of them? Our consulting physicians will make the necessary repairs. Our duty to all, as the late Charles Besson liked to phrase it, our duty, as I was saying, is to prime for the grind. *(Laughter in the room.)* This is no laughing matter.

In cases of serious breakdown, a prosthetic valve in combination with a pacemaker could be considered.

We must specify at this point that the Company will not be towing any wrecks.

Advice on maintenance will be freely supplied during consultations. But starting today, you are being advised to:

- Take a shower once you have finished work. Dust and sweat bring you down to the level of animals.
- Protect your most valuable tools: your hands. Your hands are enlarged and deformed. Their skin is rough and repulsive to the touch. Slather them with moisturizing cream. By doing this you

will avoid unsightly calluses. Then you can chastise your wives and children with big, solid, blemish-free paws. But permit me a word of advice, gentlemen: whenever possible, spare your spouses! Where would you be without them?

- Rid yourselves of bad habits. Don't talk! We are forever repeating and re-repeating this. Must we blare it in your ears? Pointless talk drives men insane. It's a well known fact.
- Gentlemen, your faces are pale and sickly. Your expressions are blank. You seem dazed. Some of you are ready to drop from fatigue. Others are staggering along pathetically. Straighten up! Show a little spirit for God's sake! The army made men, capital M, out of you. Men of character. Make sure you stay that way!
- Concentrate. Pay attention to your work. Don't allow yourself to be stupidly distracted by your fellow workers. One false move and the rolling mills can tear your hands off. Everyday, nincompoops get their fingers or hands ripped away. You'd think they were doing it on purpose! The clock-watchers among you will stop at nothing to get out of working. This much we know. But we are not given to suspicion here. Trust and openness are the words we live by.

Have any of our entreaties, dear friends, had any effect on you? We doubt it. You are so rash. But it is our mission to keep pursuing our credo: work, work, work!

No one will deny that excessive work can lead inferior subjects to their deaths. It can happen. But let me reassure you right away. Places left vacant by deceased persons are instantly filled. And our factory does not suffer, so to speak, from these minor setbacks.

Control your movements, gentlemen. You are not synchronized. This is unfortunate. It does seem to us sometimes that

The Award

you aren't putting all the passion and joy you are capable of into your work. My goodness, what an imperfect creature man is!

EXPERIENCE THE SPIRITUAL DIMENSION OF YOUR WORK!
Experience the spiritual dimension of your work and, as you feel yourself transported, your body will soon follow suit.

Rectify as rapidly as possible the pathetic uselessness of your left limbs by developing them with a variety of exercises. You must break through this absurd division of the human body that only allows you to achieve half your potential. What a waste, when you think of it!

In order to increase the already incredible level of your performance, we urge you to register without delay in our work-fitness training programs. This experiment, which has been ongoing for several months, has yielded conclusive results. Thanks to a method using electrical stimulation, you will learn, among a thousand other things, how to rid yourself of useless and superfluous gestures: scratching, digging, false maneuvers, exploration of various orifices, unusual movements of the extremities in general, exercises in testicular traction currently observed in our native population. With the aid of communication and dialogue you will be initiated into the practice of work without protest. We have a great deal of confidence in dialogue.

ELEVATE DIALOGUE, ERADICATE IDLENESS
We hope, ladies and gentlemen, that your factory will be the place where you blossom, the fertile soil where your creative potential will emerge, grow and prosper. As the great people's poet wrote, the factory is the future of man. In this we must rejoice.

THE FACTORY IS THE FUTURE OF MAN

In business, unfortunately, opportunities to rejoice are few. Our work is so all consuming that it doesn't allow us to join together in celebration as often as we'd like.

The event that brings us together today is exceptional since it involves the presentation of the work medals to the finest among you. It is with unconcealed happiness that I now turn my attention to our first medal recipient, Mr. Augustus Donte.

From the time you first entered our Company, my dear Mr. Donte, you have enjoyed the confidence and respect of all. Your modest demeanor, your professionalism—which I wouldn't hesitate to qualify with hyperbole—in close connivance with your devotion and your loyalty, classed you right away among our most brilliant workers.

Entirely dedicated to the factory's cause, you are bold in action, impetuous in work, but always polite and amiable towards your superiors. Your foremen are quick to praise your self-effacing character. Everyone here likes you and calls you Gus. Let's face it. The factory is your second home.

You have imbued your children Pierre and Nicolas with a sense of duty and submission to the natural hierarchies. Your oldest son Pierre has joined you in our Consortium. We hope one day to welcome your grandsons and—why not—your great-grandsons as well.

On behalf of your fellow workers, your superiors and Ourself, we personally award you this silver medal with our most sincere congratulations.

(Applause)

MEDAL RECIPIENT'S RESPONSE

I thank you with all my heart for this silver medal. It is the answer to my prayers and the crowning achievement of my twenty years of work life. *(Mr. Augustus Donte expresses himself in a particularly loud voice. This is a habit he acquired in his workshop because of the noise level.)*

I joined the factory the day after my wedding. I was twenty-two years old. The night before, I got shitfaced drunk. My wife was crying. My mother as well. She was calling me her baby. Between sniffles she kept saying, "I'm losing you, I'm losing you." Emotion was at its peak. I had only one thought in mind and that was leaving. I may have been a newlywed but I was already thinking ahead. After this memorable night, I went down to the hiring office. Driven by my wife and my mother who were still sniveling. Women always end up winning. Just by whining.

At the factory, I was put through all sorts of tests. They wanted to find out who the real me was. They asked me if I was divorced, Jewish, polygamous, if I was a Communist, if I didn't by any chance have a Communist friend, or a Communist parent, "try to remember," or some vague Communist association, "think it over carefully and answer honestly, it's important," if I had ever been in prison with experienced killers who were spreading slacker propaganda, "and while we are on the subject, what do you think about leisure?" "I have the leisure to think," I said. "Aha! this man has spirit." They probed my depths. Examined my pedigree. They checked out my instincts, inspected my idiosyncrasies, and rooted out my darkest secrets. Because I was free of defects, you had the decency to take me on. Of course when I say "you," it's because I can't say precisely who it was that did the hiring. Because at that time, there was no Director of Human Resources. It's by details like this that you can measure progress.

I was put on the night shift. In the pit. I got to work and back on foot, so I could save on bus tickets. Hoofed it for two kilometers to get myself in shape. I was alone on my job. The assembly line was in full swing. The car moved forward. I was underneath, in the pit. I'd lift my left hand, quick. I'd whack the support plate onto the frame, fast, to protect the anchor points of the torsion bars. With my right hand, I'd put a screw into the tip of the drill. Then I'd lift the drill. And presto, I'd screw the thing into place. Often, I'd blow it. The support plate would fall. I'd lose my screws. I'd be groping around for them along the edges of the hole above my head. Another car would come. I'd panic. Everything would start piling up in front and in back. I'd hear the guys swearing. The foreman would look at me like I was a complete moron. When the whistle blew, two thirds of the support plates wouldn't be in place. I was sinking fast. It was awful. The noise was terrible. A never-ending screech, with other screeches mixed in. I was going insane in this screeching darkness. It was night when I went to work. It was night when I left to go home. It was always night, not just outside but in my head as well. I thought I'd go crazy from lack of sunlight. And when I say crazy, I mean crazy. In my sleep deprived state, the machines would take on a life of their own. They'd seem cruel and twisted to me. My life had become this endless gray blur of terror. And then I became the terror.

At home, I insisted on total silence. My nerves were shot.

The Award

The slightest noise would send me right over the edge. One angry morning, I killed the neighbor's dog with a swift kick to the jaw. His barking was boring into my skull. This act, that people around here were pompous enough to call a crime, caused me no end of trouble. Because people around here feel about dogs in a way I simply can't figure out. It's ridiculous.

For the information of those who, like me, can't stand these pests: one good kick to the schnozz and you'll send the mutt on a non-stop flight to doggie heaven. No touchdowns. Let me just add that I hope God in his mercy thought of separate camps in heaven for dogs and men. If he didn't, we may as well go to hell. We'd be less out of our element there anyhow. *(Mr. Donte's jokes obtain no response from the audience)*

Getting back to the noise, I couldn't tolerate it—none. My kids' screaming sent me into fits of rage. I'd hit them. It was my only release in that sickening life. A few whacks with the buckle side of the belt and I'd feel a lot better. I'd generally aim for the legs and the backside. I was a good shot. But sometimes in the heat of the action, I'd miss my target and the belt would hit somebody's face. Then my wife would start screaming "not the head! not the head!" Then I'd hit her too. So she'd shut up.

On some blessed days, the simple act of undoing my belt and seeing the fear in the kid's eyes would be enough to calm me down. There was also the fact that my arms were causing me unbelievable pain and each movement increased my suffering. Repeating the same movement all night long made my hands swell up and left my armpits blazing. I'd be holding my arms out like a penguin. It was grotesque.

My wife would take advantage of this. She had the heart and

soul of a nurse. She was attracted to all types of wounds. Especially mine. The redder, the better. She'd have given anything to dust my armpits with talcum powder the way I'd seen her do it on my kid's behinds. I resisted. Her treatments made me sick. Anything my wife did involving children's hygiene I always found incredibly disgusting. And the pleasure she takes in sniffing and fiddling with infant excrement always seemed like some kind of perversion to me.

All women like baby poop. A lot more than old people's. To each his own. As for me, having the innermost recesses of my body dusted with talcum powder like some kid's shit-covered behind was total humiliation. Especially since my wife would take advantage and reverse the situation between us. She degraded me with her treatments. She'd make me into her little darling, her patient. With those ass-wiping hands she'd cut me down to size. With that stomach-turning sweetness she castrated me. I'd give in to her from sheer exhaustion. She'd turn it into a victory. Inside, she knew she had it over me. It was her way of getting even.

I was dominated by my wife at home and by my foreman at the factory. I was dominated by the machines in the workshop, and by time and exhaustion. I was no longer in control of my life. It was slipping through my fingers like sand.

There wasn't one day during this awful period when I felt normally healthy, normally free and normally strong. I was constantly beat up and irritated. But worst of all, I couldn't resign myself to this atrocious life that not even an animal would've put up with. But I couldn't escape from it either. Because there were children that had to be fed, and my wife who would have

The Award

slowly died of grief, I guess, if I had taken off to Kazakhstan, like I dreamed of doing. And regrets, I didn't want.

I'd been taken by force into a life I hadn't chosen. Pushed along like some animal in a herd that has no idea where it's going. I was chained to the production line like a slave in the olden days. In a pit, to boot. In the twentieth century, in France! You'd never believe it if you read it in a book. So I told myself to hang on. "Hang on if you're a real man," this is what I told myself every day. And I held on until the next day when I'd repeat the same thing to myself again. It went on like this for years.

In spite of what my wife might have wanted to achieve by shoving all that mothering down my throat, which was just her way of trying to castrate me, she never managed to make me kowtow to her. I wasn't the least bit nice to her. "You poor dumb cluck," I'd say, instead of yes or no. "Shut up, you dumb cluck." And I never gave her any credit for her culinary creations, which were her only joy in life, because my wife, I must admit, is the uncontested queen of omelets, she could make an omelet from nothing, she could have made an omelet out of stones if she couldn't find anything else, and as for paella, she came close to genius. But instead of dishing out some praise like I should have ... "It's inedible," I'd holler, then I'd push the plate away in a fury even if I was dying of hunger, which made me even more irritable. "I'm sick of your shit!" I'd scream at her like some invalid. Then she'd put on her victim's face and I'd feel like cracking her across the jaw just to see that martyred look disappear. "Don't give me that martyr stuff," I'd yell at her, slamming the door behind me, "You're driving me nuts!"

So then my wife would start to sniffle and sob. And I'd say to myself, Hey, you expect a little comfort and silence and instead you get moaning and tears. And the more I heard my wife sniffle and sob, the madder I got. At her. At me. At the whole universe.

Love is incompatible with work. That's why it's a rare thing, if you ask me.

One morning, I got on my moped. I didn't know where I was going. Sky's the limit once you allow yourself to believe it. I rode all day. Into the clear.

No more wife, no more kids, no more leash around my neck. No more foreman up my ass. I pissed where I felt like it. On sunflowers, or I'd aim it up into the sky in a gesture of defiance. It was a little silly but it did me good. I was alone. I felt good. I was waking up from a night that had lasted for years. I felt free.

I ended up in the Vaucluse. How I landed there, I don't know. It was the month of June. The earth smelled good. I found work on a building site. I learned how to be a construction worker. I built the Lauris Post Office and Cabrière School. I felt at home on the scaffold. I liked being suspended in midair with a bird's eye view of things. It's easier to whistle at girls from high up than from down below. Especially when you're shy like me. It was up there that I got a taste for heights that has lasted till this day.

I stayed in a two-bit boarding house with other lost souls like myself. The bit of money I did make I tossed out the window. I remember a redhead with an huge ass who spent hours making my bed. Until I'd get all hot and bothered. You can figure out the rest. One Sunday in June, I saw the sea for the first time. The beach of Sainte-Mariès was empty. I almost cried. It was my first artistic experience.

Two years after I'd gone, my mother wrote me a letter that

The Award

began, "My dear departed son." As if I was dead. The rest was a lot of wailing piled onto blame, threats—more or less veiled—and morbid fantasies. My absence was killing her. She only had one wish: to see the light of her life before her body was packed into a coffin, which wouldn't be a long time coming. And at the end of her masterpiece, the way she howled for me was pure poetry. Me, I'd always been able to resist that deformed body of hers, but I couldn't resist her piercing cries. I obeyed her summons. I went home. When it comes to a son's duty, I'm a pushover.

I have to say that my mother, despite her legendary nastiness and deformed breasts, has always had a magnetic influence over me, an irresistible pull that I've never figured out, and it usually lands me into trouble. And sure enough. I knew right away when I got home. My goose was cooked.

I went back to my job at the factory. In the same shop. With the same noise. The same gloomy faces. The same pictures of naked women on the lockers in the changing room, with the same big tits and cocksucker lips. I went back home. My kennel was waiting. Nice and clean. My wife didn't say a word. That came much later, during her change of life. They say it's normal. Old grudges come back. Twenty-year-old grudges, deep-frozen and completely intact. Unbelievable spite, perfectly preserved. A treasure trove of resentments built up day after day, a small fortune's worth. My children got long in the face as soon as they saw me. The youngest one started howling. I held myself back from shutting his trap in one blow. My wife looked at me with nervous eyes. The eyes of a dog you've just whistled for. She put on her hurt look. She never quit putting it on. It became her true face. The other face, the old one, disappeared for good. It was like my wife had been replaced by a woman whose features sometimes brought back flashes of a long dead love. We sat down to eat. There was veal in white sauce. She served me veal in white sauce after two years absence! I nearly lost it. But I didn't say anything. I turned on the TV. The weather channel announced rain for the north half of the country. I was back in my rut.

Now I'm in the swing of it. It's going fine. You can get used to anything. Even the worst. As long as you manage to stay alive.

In my twenty years of service, I haven't been laid off once. Not one messy scene. Never a raised voice. I do my work, period, from start to finish. I look down on the ones who spend hours hiding out in the johns. That kind of stuff is degrading. Cheating never brings anyone anything. Only trouble and shame.

With my bosses, I keep my trap shut. If you give 'em any lip it always works against you. I learned that one ages ago. The important thing at the factory is not to attract attention to yourself. To blend in with the walls. Gray of heart and gray of skin. All you have to do is what you're told. Very nicely. And hang onto your job like an exhausted swimmer to a drifting tree, to use a little poetry.

I've never joined in a strike. I don't want to be mistaken for a fool. Like my Uncle Louis would say: better to roll in shit than in your own illusions. Shit at least you can wash off, sorry for getting so graphic. And speaking of illusions! All the delegates want to do is give themselves airs and make a lot of noise while they quietly scheme for a few lousy advantages. Their dream is to be on top. Just like the others. Me, I don't want to be at anyone's beck and call, thank you very much. And as for solidarity, I don't believe in it. In the shop, there isn't any. No union. No

The Award

friendship. Nothing. Just people fighting all night long over the stupidest things. It's "go fuck yourself" or "go to hell" every time someone tries to bring something up. We get fed up in the end. Everyone keeps to themselves. It's less risky. And if by some fluke we do get a real discussion going about bosses and politics, the moment we start getting just a little bit closer, some snitch always rats on us. It's like clockwork.

In spite of what you think, it's very difficult to make friends at the factory. Worker solidarity is all bullshit. A delegate lie. For example, one morning I drove Paco home. He's a Portuguese who slogs away on the same assembly line as me. A nice guy. He'd missed his bus. For some time now, I've been banging around in an old wreck. Now that I'm getting older, I like to take it easy. We shot the breeze a bit, about this and that, nothing much, about our sons who play rugby, big strapping guys built like tanks. All of a sudden, we're smack in the middle of the country. He says, "Let me off here." I look around. There was, as they say, not a soul in sight. It was a desert. I didn't understand. But I didn't dare say anything. I was afraid I'd offended him with some dumb thing I'd said. He got out. I still didn't know what was going on. Then afterwards I understood. Out of some kind of pride, Paco didn't want me to see the dive he lived in.

That's why I say it's very difficult to make friends at the factory, because without trust, there's no friendship and without friendship, there's no solidarity. It's simple logistics.

But I'm not cursing my fate, like so many others. I get my satisfaction. When I got promoted from OS to P1, I had a real sense of personal pride. You really feel the difference in your standard of living.

When my wife starts griping, I tell her as long as I'm still standing and we don't owe anything, we've got nothing to complain about. I only hope I can hang on till retirement.

(The end of Mr. Augustus Donte's account is greeted with applause. The Director of Human Resources waits for silence before taking the microphone.)

I want to thank Mr. Augustus Donte who has, in simple and poignant language, managed to convey his gratitude. As he so nicely pointed out in his charming speech, our factory wouldn't be what it is today without the dynamic presence of our Division Heads. I now have the pleasure of turning the microphone over to Mr. Protte, our exuberant Director of Human Relations, who will continue to outline our new set of reforms.

SECOND SPEECH

Ladies and gentlemen,

The age of misery is over. *Germinal, L'Assommoir.* all of this is in the past. Finito! We have entered a new era. The future is at our doorstep. We are saying yes to rapid expansion. Yes to social progress. Yes to rapid social progress. We are sailing way ahead of the competition. Look us up in the directory and you will find us listed under Winner! And we're proud of it.

But despite our solicitude and willingness to exchange, we have noted with displeasure that some of you, a rare few thank God, are displaying nasty and incredibly impudent behavior. Is this the thanks we get? Human ingratitude has no limits! Gentlemen, we are making a thousand efforts to please you and we want you to do the same. This kind of aggression becomes tiresome after awhile. We don't know what to do with you anymore! Fortunately, we do have our experts! Our experts have an answer for everything. Based on their proposals, we have instituted special courses on friendship. What can be more wonderful than friendship between human beings! "For me, nothing is more beautiful and nothing is more valuable than the bloom of a rose and the love of a friend . . ." Ladies and gentlemen, these courses are free. We cordially invite you to register for them.

Sessions in psychodrama are also being offered. Come one, come all. You will act out your violent feelings towards your superiors by attacking leather dummies. These dummies have easily recognizable faces. Mine, I must admit, is very true to life. Well, except maybe the ears . . . At the end of each session, our consultant in industrial psychology will take you aside to explain the forces that motivate your aggression as well as your innate desire for unhappiness.

We are engaged, ladies and gentlemen, in an ongoing battle against your innate desire for unhappiness. But we are tenacious. We never surrender to discouragement. Your well-being is dear to our hearts and, if necessary, we will impose it upon you.

To better combat the noise of our machines, our engineers have perfected a musical hard hat that is very becoming and specially adapted to your working conditions. It will be compulsory to wear these hats. Anyone who breaks the rules will be punished. You have been forewarned. Spare the rod and spoil the child. This invention which combines practicality with pleasure is just one among thousands of examples of our commitment to progress. We want progress, progress, and more progress! And to provide you with immediate and irrefutable proof of this, I am delighted to announce, ladies and gentlemen, the upcoming construction of a new company restaurant.

This restaurant will hold two thousand. The atmosphere will be subdued and conducive to intimacy. Pink, which promotes harmony, will be the dominant tone. You will feel right at home. Loudspeakers will permanently broadcast soft music. The old family-style tables will be replaced by small modern ones. And on each one, a lovely plastic bouquet.

THE SAME RESTAURANT FOR ALL

The same restaurant for all. At the same price for all. No inequality! We detest inequality! Detest, detest, detest it!

In this charming, cozy setting, you will be able to converse

The Award

pleasantly with your superiors. Your superiors are always ready to engage in open frank communication. Reserve them your warmest welcome.

At our insistence, our engineers, who have been complaining about your disgusting displays of openmouthed chewing, our engineers, as I was saying, have promised to contain their revulsion. So, be nice! Break the ice!

And now, since I have the opportunity, I would like to verify some information that strikes me as altogether preposterous. Is it true that certain workers prefer eating the cold, unappetizing contents of their lunch boxes to sharing their meal with us in friendship? Well? Must I interpret this silence as confirmation? This is absolutely stupefying!

And this isn't the worst of it! Our informers have learned from confirmed sources that these same workers have been displaying hostility towards their supervisors, hostility that borders on phobia in a few exceptional cases. Gentlemen, we are astonished. And pained. Profoundly pained. Because your supervisors, after all, do not dispute your privileges in the least. Not one of them covets your many advantages. Quite the contrary! They do the utmost to ensure that you stay put in your jobs. So don't be difficult. And for goodness sakes, retract those claws!

We would like to see an end to this perpetual recrimination, which truly spoils the warm ambiance of our Home. But this seems practically impossible. Our experts are categorical. A worker is characterized by two major insurmountable flaws: one, he doesn't know how to keep still, two, he doesn't know how to keep quiet. You can be sure of one thing every day. That type of worker (I am not referring to you of course but to the "ordinary" worker, if I dare say so), that type of worker is afflicted with the annoying habit of protesting. At the drop of a hat he blames, he demands, he complains. Like a woman he is never happy. It's maddening. His parents, grandparents and great grandparents were illiterate bumpkins of unparalleled crudeness who did not teach him the ordinary rules of etiquette. And that worker is ignorant of the fact that, among respectable people, to protest or complain is in extremely poor taste.

Ladies and gentlemen, learn to say yes. Say yes without hesitating to our self-improvement program. It was conceived for your benefit. Develop your ability to accept. Introductory courses on consent are being organized in Aix-en-Provence for the modest sum of six thousand francs. At the end of these sessions the most rebellious among you will know how to just say: Yes!

JUST SAY YES!
Must we drum it in yet again? You do not, gentlemen, have any cause to complain. We guard against all contingencies. If there is one thing we cannot stand, it's contingencies. At any rate, our Chief Executive Officer does not receive any complaints. He is available to no one. Our Chief Executive Officer hates to be interrupted. He is devoted to his accounts. Passionately so. And he works tirelessly to increase your happiness.

For our Chief Executive Officer just loves to do good. And his wife is just like him. Extremely humanitarian. When the missus is not doing good, the missus gets bored. Then she has to go to her psychoanalyst five times a week. At four hundred francs a session, that's a salary in itself!

The Award

The Chief Executive Officer and his close collaborators are interested only in assuring you the peace of mind and joy to which you are entitled but which malevolent individuals are bent on destroying with their insidious declarations.

Certain agitators, whose messages are spread daily by the tabloids, actually claim that in the future man will be replaced by the machine. We energetically decry these vicious untruths. No, no, no! Man is in every way superior to the machine. We give you our word.

Taking great care to remain both alert and objective, we have reflected on the respective advantages and disadvantages of man and the machine.

All things considered, one thing is clear: Man is much less costly than the machine.

He is also adaptable and can be endlessly improved. The added feature of a conscience makes all the difference. Have you ever seen a machine tortured by remorse and hellbent on doing better? Have you ever seen a machine, bitten by the venom of ambition, increase its energy by tenfold? Don't make me laugh!

Man is pliable, controllable, and extremely sophisticated, I believe, infinitely more sophisticated than the machine, all while remaining extremely simple to use.

Like the machine, he is carnivorous and kills in cold blood when necessity demands it.

In general, he deteriorates much more slowly than the latter. Rare is the machine that functions longer than forty years without requiring costly repairs.

A true worker should, in a sense, be a symbol of all the qualities I have just listed but . . . please excuse me.

(The Director of Human Relations reads the sheet that the Head of Security has just slipped into his hand.)

Ladies and gentlemen, we have just been informed that in Workshop 18, workers in the throes of collective insanity have abandoned their tools to spray each other with water and spit at each other while laughing uproariously. Some, it seems are strolling about, grotesquely coiffed in women's shower caps. It's pathetic! You have to be totally devoid of any company spirit to indulge in this kind of buffoonery. At home is one thing, but in public! A particularly repulsive gob of black spittle landed on the face of our Chief Engineer, Mr. Colonna, who was passing by. It's a disgrace!

These actions, ladies and gentlemen, are intolerable and deserve severe punishment. We will not tolerate one more minute of the havoc these enemies of progress are wreaking in our little hive.

But misfortune has its purposes! We are in fact happy to note that our most devoted workers immediately sounded the alarm and turned in the guilty parties. We warmly congratulate them. For greater convenience, denouncement forms will be distributed. These special forms are anonymous. However, if the applicant wants to receive his little bonus, he must include his name, surname and address.

My dear Miss Pizzuto, we will not be asking you for your name, or your address, as we have known you since the first flush of your youth. We might as well say forever. If my memory serves me correctly *(the Director of Human Relations checks his file)*, you joined us on July 17, 1968.

From the time you arrived, your devotion, self-sacrifice, and

The Award

your inordinate desire for work distinguished you right away as a highly skilled worker.

In every circumstance, you have demonstrated admirable self-denial. And if the labor to which you give yourself body and soul is sometimes a trial for your hands, it always remains a joy for your heart.

You are being repaid for your zeal today, my dear Miss Pizzuto, since we have the immense pleasure of decorating you with the vermilion medal.

We want to make it clear to our amiable audience that the medal presentations are not to be sullied by the addition of any financial supplement. We resist, at every step of the way, the infatuation with money and misappropriation of public funds that has run rampant in our country for several years now.

MEDAL RECIPIENT'S RESPONSE

No one told me I'd have to make a speech. I thought you just said thank you and that was it. I don't know what to say in front of all these people. *(Miss Pizzuto wipes her tear-stained cheeks with both hands, while in the second-to-last row, her mother and sister dab their faces with tissues.)* O.K., may as well take the plunge. I'll just have to make the best of it. *(Miss Pizzuto holds her arms straight out as if she is about to take the plunge in earnest, to the great amusement of those in the first rows.)*

I can say it now that he's dead. My father was a monster. He was the cause of all our problems. He ended up destroying the few people who stuck by him over the years. He destroyed my mother for real and he also destroyed my sister by turning her against my mother in a scene you would not have believed, a scene straight from hell. He destroyed me in a way as well, but I ended up getting out of it. He hit and punished my sister and me on a regular basis. And he beat up on my mother any time she crossed him. All his life, he terrorized us, my mother, my sister and me, especially when he was smashed, which happened at least once a week, and then you had to watch out 'cause he sent everything flying, the chairs, the plates, the knickknacks, and us along with them. And all his life he took advantage of the fact that we were terrified of him to get what he wanted from us, but with me it never worked a hundred percent, and he never forgave me for that. And even in his last moments, when he was only a doddering, senile old wreck who did it in his pants, he still went after us, my mother, my sister and me, and he'd spit out the vilest things he could come up with just to make sure he could still get to us. He got such a kick out of it. He was probably just so pleased that his nastiness was still in such good working order even though the rest of him had fallen to wrack and ruin. But Daddy, who I despised more than anything in the whole wide world, because he made me feel like the lowest thing in the whole wide world, he did me one big favor: in a way, he forced me, at age 16, to get out of the house where I was born, away from him.

It was on the night of July 14 that it happened. My mother had begged my father all day to let me go to the ball. At nine o'clock, Claudette Lizat came to get me. My father finally gave in. "Go and be a slut if that's what you want!" It was hot. The orchestra was playing "Une belle histoire." I was dancing with Michel Cazelle, the hardware dealer's son. He was trying to press his cheek against mine. He was moving very slowly towards his goal. I could feel his breath against my skin. It gave me such a funny feeling. I'd been waiting for this moment to come for months, like some miracle, and now that it was happening, all it did was give me a funny feeling. All of a sudden, I saw my father slicing through the crowd in my direction. I knew right away what he was going to do. But I didn't budge. I kept right on dancing with Michel Cazelle as if nothing was happening. I didn't pull away. I squeezed his hand harder to give myself courage. And when my father came up to me, I looked him straight in the eye knowing perfectly well what he was going to do, that what he was going to do would be disastrous . . . But I didn't make one move to stop him. I didn't take off running and I didn't scream before he hit me, the way I usually did. My father yanked me violently by the

The Award

shoulder and whacked me across the face so hard I thought my jaw would be dislocated. The couples dancing around us stopped dead in their tracks. Michel Cazelle got such a stupid look on his face. And at that very moment I stopped loving him. At that very moment. I didn't cry. I didn't show the least sign of emotion. I didn't react for a few moments. Then I walked home with my head held high. And the second I went through the door, at that exact same second, I said to myself: right, enough is enough, tomorrow you'll pack your bags and then it's so long! Once you rough it, twice you tough it, three you stuff it. And the next day I cleared out. At the time this was a very strange move to make and it was a shameful thing for the parents. But I didn't even give it a thought. I turned my back on my family. I turned my back on my village, I turned my back on everything I knew in life. I left empty-handed, like Jesus. No diploma, no money, nothing. That's how I ended up at the factory overnight. Me, who dreamed of being a stewardess!

The few first months were rough, believe me. It's true when they say that the first steps are the hardest. The smell of rubber made me nauseous. My fingers were raw. I had pain in the back of my neck and all the way down my arms. But it was the noise that was the worst. It was like a constant assault on the brain. My brain felt like this huge raw wound that got ripped open by every sound wave. It felt like I had a bumblebee trapped inside of my head and it was bouncing nonstop off the sides of my skull, bam off one side, bam off the other, bam on one side, bam on the other.

And to top it off, there was Tronchin, the foreman who circled around me all day long. The dwarf, they called him. And no wonder. He barely stood four and a half feet tall. Some people thought this explained his nastiness. Maybe it did, but in my opinion, it was still no excuse. I had that dwarf hot on my heels every single minute at work, with his platform shoes that sort of made him walk like a cripple. He never let up all fucking day! What a nightmare! A dwarf in love with me! I never had much luck in love, that's for sure!

I should tell you that at age 16 I wasn't deformed like I am now. I was more what you'd call a looker. I had this inexplicable power over men. Actually it was more like a supernatural power considering the getup I had on. It's true, I was pretty stacked . . . but that still didn't explain the whole mystery. The fact was, I had this miniature foreman, if you'll excuse the expression, right on my tail the whole time like some sniffing dog! I had to peel him off me like a leech!

I had no choice but to put up with it. No way I could have sent him packing. Because at the time the foremen did whatever they wanted to you. I'm talking about the old days, twenty years ago, what am I saying, twenty-five years ago, twenty-five, that's right, since I got the vermilion medal, what an idiot. Things have changed a lot since then. But at the time, if I'd made a fuss, Tronchin could have sent me to a punishment station with nasty machines that had skulls and crossbones on them and smells to match. So I kept my mouth shut. And the words piled up inside me. And they weighed me down like stones.

But Tronchin wasn't the only one who kept pestering me, and that's putting it nicely. In 1968, I was the only woman in the workshop, a pioneer is what *Besson* magazine called me. Talk about a privilege! As soon as I'd get there, a hundred pairs of eyes would

The Award

zoom in on me, a hundred pairs of bulging eyes taking in all the nice round juicy parts of my body, first the front, then the back like I was the cheapest of sluts. My legs would start to give. My whole body would start to shake. I'd wish the factory would burn to the ground, that some disaster would happen, that everything would collapse and never be heard from again. Me, who no man had ever touched since the ball episode, suddenly I was having to deal with lechery that was worse than being groped. But I'd just keep walking down the center aisle like a machine, with all those looks clamped onto my private parts. It was torture.

At this point there was always some moron who'd start tossing obscenities at me as I went by, unbelievable filth that I could never repeat, disgusting smut that made everyone else crack up. It was their way of unwinding. Filthy jokes gave them a really good laugh. It was about the only thing that did make them laugh. Me, I just kept going down the center aisle, trying as hard as I could to disappear inside myself, so to speak, to see nothing and hear nothing. Like a robot.

One day, a fellow worker who never opened his mouth came to my defense. It took guts. He gave them a long-winded speech with words from the Bible. He ended it by telling them that by degrading me they were degrading themselves. This kept them quiet for a few days. Then they started up again, worse than ever. In the end I just got used to it.

In the beginning, I'd start at 5 A.M. and leave at 1:00 in the afternoon. The bus would let me off in front of my door. I'd drag myself up the stairs to the sixth floor. The stairs stank of ammonia. I'd sit down on my bed. I felt more dead than alive. I had no strength left in me, no strength left for anything. I didn't even have the strength left to cry, because you need at least a bit of energy to feel your unhappiness and cry. It was cold. It was that winter when it was so cold. I'd go to bed. Trouble was, the minute I'd get to sleep, I'd dream I was back on the assembly line covering seats. I'd be pulling the seat cover over the frame, I'd be stretching the fabric over the four corners and pressing down on the snaps with my thumbs—that's the part that hurt the most. Then I'd start the same thing all over again with another seat. I'd pull the cover over the frame, I'd stretch the fabric over the four corners and I'd press down on the snaps with my thumbs and so on and so forth until it was time to get up.

For years and years I dreamed every night that I was on the assembly line covering seats, pulling the cover over the frame, stretching the fabric over the four corners and pressing down on the snaps with my thumbs.

My fingers ached. I'd wrap them in rags. They'd become completely unfit for contact with other people. Unfit for touch. The idea filled me with despair. What's a life if you can't even have a simple pleasure like stroking someone's face? I thought about it all the time. My fingers weren't fit for much, period. In order to eat, I had to hold the cutlery between my swollen fingers like some cripple. And if I felt like smoking at break time, I had to pull the cigarette out of the pack with my teeth. Like a monkey.

I'd get up. I'd still be exhausted. As exhausted as if I'd lifted the entire earth with my own two arms. No joke. I'd listen to the radio. I'd read romance novels. Or I'd do nothing. Most of the time I'd do nothing. I'd sit on my bed, like an idiot. The smell of rubber was permanently stuck to my skin. I'd drench myself with cologne. The smell of rubber stayed. I'd open the window.

The Award

Night would be falling. I'd make myself dinner. I'd demolish it. I'd eat like an animal. Sometimes when I'd catch myself eating like an animal, I'd get scared. In that split second I'd tell myself, lady, you're killing yourself, you're going to keel over and die if you keep on going like this, you'll never make it at this rate. I saw my youth fading before me, if that period of horrible loneliness where all my juice was sucked dry in one shot can be called youth. I'd make resolutions. Tomorrow, I'd say, you're going to settle up, then it's goodbye. Then I'd dream about another life, where pleasure was part of the game, where time wasn't clocked like we were running a marathon, where people ate peacocks in china dishes. I don't even know if peacocks exist, if they're for real or what, personally I think they're the product of someone's imagination. Then right away I'd become lethargic again. I was so exhausted, so drained of willpower, that any thought that came to me I'd just let die.

On the assembly line I didn't speak to anyone. I'm not one for confiding in people. I'm always afraid of intruding. As it was, I was stuck between a Portuguese, I've forgotten his name, it'll come back to me, and a gigantic Yugoslav, Petro they called him. There wasn't much potential for chitchat there.

The only one I would have liked to confide in was Christian Laurence, an Ardéchois who had been to university and who could have gone far in life, become an engineer or maybe even something better, if his luck hadn't run out. They said he was writing some kind of novel about the factory. Frankly, I don't see what you could find to say about the factory. Could you find anything thrilling to tell about seat covering or window installation? Why not write a novel about me while you're at it! I know I sound like

I'm making fun of him, but it's quite the opposite. Christian Laurence seemed so superior to me, I hardly dared open my mouth in front of him. Everything about him, his black scarf, that romantic flair, the way he had of using big words without sounding crass, everything about him seemed superior.

The others made his life hell, for the sake of revenge. They were quick to figure out that brains and education just work against a man when he's on the wrong side of the tracks. And it was true that Christian Laurence's beautiful speeches were no match for the viciousness of that prick Tronchin. The workers wouldn't give him a break. They made fun of him. They imitated his mannerisms, which were almost the mannerisms of a woman. "Mr. Laurence, would you be so kind as to pass me a screwdriver?" They never got tired of proving that brains and education are completely useless against ridicule. They treated him like they would some dumb chick. Christian Laurence never fought back. And if he got started on one of his elegant speeches full of difficult words that came as naturally to him as breathing ... "Whoa there queer boy, cut the bullshit, you're not at school here!" and then they'd burst out laughing. Christian Laurence would go all pale. But his discomfort would just get them all going and they'd start provoking him all over again. They'd hide his tools. They'd watch him get all messed up with his covers and they'd think it was hysterical. "What good are your diplomas now, moron!" They hated him instinctively.

I never said a thing. I was smart enough to know that in situations like this, the best thing to do is keep quiet. I'd just keep on working. A seat. Then another one. Then another. I was going full out. I gave it my all. In trimming, it was me who did the

The Award

most. It was me, a woman, who whipped through the most seat covers. It drove some of them crazy. We had to cover an average of seventy seats a day, and I would do seventy-five, eighty-five, peaking at ninety when I felt particularly inspired. I was possessed by a demon, that's the only explanation. I couldn't stop myself. I was working myself to death with a rage I didn't understand. I was crashing full speed ahead. Without looking up. Without looking back. Like a tank.

The delegates came to threaten me on a regular basis. "Hey, whoa there, slow down baby! Cool it, or we'll have to cool you!" But I didn't listen, I couldn't. My life was work and nothing else. I wasn't doing it for bonuses, though I admit they're nothing to spit at, or to be in the bosses' good books. I'm not like that. I did it because work was my only reason for getting up, walking, eating and going on with my life even if it was, at the same time, the reason I felt, I felt, I don't have the words to express it, how would you describe feeling like you were stuck in a desert in the middle of the city?

Then things settled down.

Now I live with Siki. When I say, "Come to mama," he comes. When I say, "Jump for mama," he jumps. When I say to him, "Now, sonny boy, you listen to your mama," he listens. I call him son. I can't help myself. I know it shocks some people. I guess it's hard to understand if you don't have a dog to love. Like Gus back there. But I don't hold it against him. He just doesn't know what he's missing, that's all. On Sundays, my doggie and I go to La Simiane Park to take in some fresh air. I've gotta say, we're a little crowded during the week. My place is tiny. Luckily, I've got a folding table and a pull-out sofa. Modern furniture is not nearly as nice as the antique stuff, but for space and convenience, what can I say, it's unbeatable. When we're in the park, I spend hours throwing him the ball. It's a good way for him to unwind. I say to him, go on, run, my little poopsie, my little treasure, catch the bally-ball, you have fun now my precious little poochie-kins, take advantage of life. He'd do anything for me. I speak to him like he was human and he understands me just like he was human. He acts just like a real human being in every way. In the morning, for example, he can't stand to see me go. As soon as he sees me slipping on my coat, he starts to cry. Just like a kid. Just so he doesn't get sad, I keep my coat hidden and I put it on outside, on the sly. At night, I make him his food. Meat, gravy, desserts, a bit of everything. He eats exactly what I eat. Maybe he is a little high cost to maintain, but when you love somebody you don't pinch pennies. I still manage to make ends meet.

When I got Siki, I wanted to get back with my parents again. Because no matter what they say, your parents are always your parents. The bottom line is, we're the same blood. But my father made some obnoxious comments about me and my dog, about our perverted relationship, was the way he put it. My father, jealous of Siki! Now I'd seen everything! But this time I didn't lose my cool. Once you start dragging Siki in, it's game over. I told him straight off the bat: "You idiot! If loving your dog means you're a pervert, then most of the world's population must be perverts!" It was the first time I'd ever called him an idiot. He was speechless. I took the opportunity to leave. That day, I burned my bridges. Now we only see each other at Christmas, along with my sister and my brother-in-law. I'm only sorry on account of my mother, whom I love with all my heart. But we phone each other

The Award

every day. She and I, we tell each other everything. Well, most things, that is.

There is one thing my mom keeps going on about. She'd like me to start seeing someone. She never stops talking about it. She never stops painting these glowing pictures of marriage. She tells me: "I don't want to leave this life before I see you settled." She says it's not about money, it's about companionship. But me, I have all the companionship I'll ever need and more, this is what I can't seem to make her understand. And anyways, at my age, it's much too late for me to dig up a husband. I'm too old for sentimentality. And who'd I end up with anyways? One of those divorced men with godawful kids! The kind of godawful kids who hate their stepmother without even knowing why! I've known brats like that. Heaven forbid! There's nothing worse in the nastiness department. Case closed. Thank you very much! I will die without having shared my life with any man, except for my father whom I consider a monster. But I have my little woof-woof who wouldn't hurt a fly and, as far as finances go, I'm hanging in there, knock on wood. *(Miss Pizzuto taps her fist at her forehead.)* I'm no big spender. I take after Mom. Mom could save money like nobody else.

That's it. That's my life story.

Thank you so much for the magnificent medal. I'll take extra special care of it. And thank you for everything you've done for me.

(Miss Pizzuto is radiant. As she returns to her seat amid thunderous applause, Miss Besson, Director of Social Services, takes one last peek at her notes before beginning her speech.)

THIRD SPEECH

Greetings to you all, my dear friends!

We are pleased to announce that we have also given some thought to your leisure time. After the grind, time to unwind! You have to know how to distract yourselves from time to time.

Our Company organizes trips. And vacation camps. With sea and sun. And sunsets like you've never seen before. Glorious red ones. We cannot urge you strongly enough to take a camera with you on these trips. You will bring back memories in living color that will brighten up your old age.

During the bus trip, our group leaders will have you singing the Company anthem in unison. The trip will be very lighthearted and entertaining. Our group leaders have more than a few tricks up their sleeves.

We ask that you remain in your groups during these excursions. Our motto here is Togetherness. This will arm you with greater fortitude when overcoming the disorientation that sometimes provokes violent panic attacks in sensitive individuals.

Ladies and gentlemen, if the terror that grips you in face of the natives is too intense, do not get off your bus. Our enthusiastic group leaders will conduct a simulated tour on board that will make you feel as if you are right there on the site among the temples and ruins. There's no point in saddling yourselves with a guide. Our group leaders know the history and geography of the countries we will be touring as well as anyone.

At our request, we have programmed your comfort right down to the tiniest details. We want you to be happy! T-shirts will be provided free of charge. The name of our Consortium appears in big yellow letters. This shirt will be your company flag. Roll-call is at 7:00 A.M. in the hotel lobby. On your marks. Get set. Departure at 7:30 sharp. Late arrivals for the Monument tours will not be tolerated.

Ladies and gentlemen, I'm sure I need not specify that these trips are educational. We are not so stupid as to confuse leisure with lollygagging about. Allotting unscheduled time is like bribing a pack of brats with candy; it is a very short-term solution to the problem. We will not stoop to that level. A wide variety of workshops will be presented every single night. It is not compulsory to attend. If the ignorant wish to stay mired in their own muck, that's their business! However, we cannot overstress the fact that it is in your best interests to participate in these events. Your spouses may accompany you. They too have a right to know how to distinguish a crankshaft from a carburetor. New information is a well-known stimulant for conjugal conversation. The bonds between you can only be strengthened as a result. Education, ladies and gentlemen, is central to a solid home life!

Money isn't everything!

As you will be able to tell from our newly reformed policy, we have definitely not forgotten your spouses. Courses in domestic science will be given every Wednesday between ten and eleven o'clock in the secretarial offices. We are anticipating a large turnout for these courses. As a matter of fact, we are counting on it. My father with his usual forbearance created this project before he departed from this world. Ladies, honor his memory and thank him with me.

The Award

We must also thank the brilliant instructors who will be introducing you to the rudiments of domestic economy. They will teach you the delicate art of using leftovers, such as the green parts of the cauliflower, which are very tasty, or potato skins. Yes ladies, not only are potato skins edible, they are very rich in vitamin B. We will take this opportunity to remind you that the potato is one of the best fuels for the worker, since it combines two remarkable qualities: low cost and high carbohydrate content. Rice and bananas can be used as a replacement, but with less success, I fear.

SPUDS ARE SPLENDID

Your instructors will also teach you to take greater care with presentation. Presentation is everything, ladies. You tend to forget this point and to favor abundance over elegance. That is a mistake. Kant provided an admirable demonstration of this fact in his third critique; the *modus estheticus* always takes precedence over the *modus logicus*. Let me translate for you: a sprig of parsley artistically arranged on top of your plate of noodles, a slice of lemon with nicely scalloped edges tastefully set on top of your pile of cabbage, and Bob's your uncle!

Thanks to our instruction, you will be able to recognize at first glance the different cuts of beef at your butcher's: prime cuts, tenderloin, tournedos, rump steak, sirloin tip, second cuts, rib steak, top round, tip roast and chuck, and third cuts, brisket, short plate, flank and skirt. These last cuts, well-seasoned, are especially suited to the metabolism of the worker.

In short, with the guidance of your instructors you will come to understand the essence of our program: how to cook without cost. Knowing how to cook without cost is an art, I repeat, an art, that cannot be improvised.

Naturally, the food must be served at a table, on clean plates. Ladies, urge your husbands to wash their hands before sitting down to eat. This basic measure is all too often neglected by our dear workers. And while they're at it, they can brush their teeth. The smiles of some are quite frankly frightening. Besides, fresh, sweet-smelling breath can only improve relations with their superiors.

Ladies, also encourage them to eat in a less voracious manner. The less one eats, the more the stomach shrinks and the less one suffers from hunger. Any idiot knows this. Our workers, in general, eat to excess. You should see them pounce on their swill. They're like animals! It's enough to make you sick! They'd better not come complaining about digestive disorders afterwards. All excess has its price. We should not be surprised to learn that our workers make up the segment of the population with the shortest life span.

ARS LONGA, VITA BREVIS

Thanks to the instruction provided, you will finally grasp the fundamental rules of hygiene. Ladies, perspiration makes it necessary to change the bed sheets at least once a week. Don't force us to elaborate. Our workers seem to be afflicted with higher-than-average levels of perspiration, which, let's not beat around the bush, are accompanied by a fouler-than-average degree of odor. For the time being, we do not know the cause of this phenomenon. In order to reduce foot perspiration and its accompanying vicious odor, we recommend that you wash your feet every day with water and a simple cleanser. Lysol, for example. Otherwise,

The Award

gentlemen, think of the displeasure our visitors experience when they enter our workshops.

And since we are on the topic of hygiene, let me now steer you towards a subject that is dear to my heart. I have only one recommendation to make. Ladies and gentlemen, get into sports!

One need only hear the word spoken to instantly grasp the inherent virtues of sports. Sports! The explosion after the sibilant! A sly seduction of an "S," then, bam, the spurt of strength! A little power-packed word that explodes in your mouth! Sports! Our factory, my friends, is making enormous efforts to promote sports. We are convinced that a great company, just like a great country, is a company that promotes sports. For sports, ladies and gentlemen, are potent, purgative, manly, invigorating and indispensable. They reinforce your will to conquer, suppress your animal instincts, protect you against the perils of abstract contemplation and they constitute man's most effective antidote to thinking. In addition, and this is not the least of its merits, it is a powerful enhancer of family spirit. It's a fact.

Subscribe to the ASA. The Aubinoise Sports Association is offering twenty of its best seats for the next soccer game to the top-rated workers. You cannot say our Company does not pamper its top-rated workers.

Report to our group leaders and register now for the many classes and activities available to you at our splendid gymnasium: Low-Impact, Cardio-Funk, Hip-Hop, Power Jam, Step, Spinning, Rubberband, Tai Chi Chuan, Tae Kwon Do, rollerblading, jogging, there's something for everyone. These exercises will get you into peak working condition. You'll get back in the harness with wings on your feet.

Thanks to these programs, you will develop skills in automatic functioning. Any movements, even the most ludicrous, can become second nature through repetition. Nothing comes to mind right now, but I know there are millions of examples out there.

Thanks to these programs, your body and soul will coexist in glorious harmony. Ladies and gentlemen, we are fierce advocates of harmony. Our environment must be harmonious. Harmony is the only ideal in life really worth fighting for and everything about our lifestyle must enhance this subtle state. Everything. A reasonable standard of living, a wholesome state of mind, arts and crafts, light reading, tasteful music . . . And since we're on the subject of music, I do not believe I am overstepping my authority by actively discouraging you from listening to jazz. The stuff is very bad for your morals.

There is other music, my dear friends, that is every bit as dynamic and cheerful. Our attention was recently drawn to an interesting initiative undertaken by our subsidiary, the DACA Company. They have recently released a song extolling the spirit of enterprise that lies dormant in all of us. Here is the refrain. *(The Director of Social Services recites the verse while energetically keeping time with her right foot.)* "Our hearts, once heavy, are light; The universe envies our lot; Let us go for the burn in our lives; Let us go for the burn on the job."

It's a catchy little tune, if I do say so myself. I took it upon myself to suggest to our Director of Human Relations that five hundred cassettes be ordered on an experimental basis. These cassettes will be widely distributed. They will liven up all of our festive occasions, like the Christmas party, our Mother's Day celebration or the retirement get-togethers that provide such pleasant distractions from the rigors of everyday

The Award

life. They will also be used to enliven the environment in certain workshops that have a tendency to lag behind. Working to music, what could be better! We still do not understand the reasons that drive certain tiresome individuals to counter this musical project, which was conceived only to inject a healthful vigor into tired and indolent souls. You've got to admit, it's a bit much! I say we make a nice clean sweep of all these rabble rousers and killjoys, these enemies of happiness! A good clean sweep!

Happiness! Just another empty word you say, a lie, an unattainable paradise, the end of the rainbow, an illusion created to lull the afflicted masses! Well, I'm telling you loud and clear: not for us it isn't!

(The Head of Security leans towards Miss Besson, Director of Social Services, and whispers something in her ear.)

My God, that's unbelievable! *(Regaining her composure.)* Ladies and gentlemen, we regret to inform you that, contrary to expectations, the agitation is spreading. Our forecasters were mistaken. Our reaction to the first indications of trouble was the product of leniency, and now just look at the results! The workers of workshop 22 have descended upon the time clocks in a state of wild disarray while making siren noises. Oh that's funny! *(Catching herself.)* These incidents, ladies and gentlemen, are un-ac-ceptable! Under no circumstances can they recur! It's too much! The troublemakers must be im-me-di-a-te-ly expelled! One must be prepared to take drastic action at a moment's notice. It would seem that once the boss stops shaking his fist, the worker inevitably slacks off. It's a law of nature.

If firmness does not suffice, we will resort to force. *Etiam fera animalia si clausa teneas virtutis obliviscentur.*

But I want to reassure you, ladies and gentlemen. Mr. Fabre, our Head of Security, assures us the surveillance cameras have permitted them to identify a large number of the seditious workers. You may be very interested to know that most of them had previously been singled out thanks to our aptitude tests which revealed, I quote, "channeling of aggression through the genitals sphere." I do not understand how something can be channeled through a sphere, but I digress. Make no mistake about it, our Control Commission will see to it that a supplementary inquiry into the activities of the guilty parties is set up without delay.

(There is another verbal exchange between the Director of Social Services and the Head of Security.)

Ladies and gentlemen, we are pleased to announce that the true workers who agree to assist us in uncovering the guilty parties and delivering them to justice will receive an additional bonus of five hundred francs from their grateful Company. The Company does not cut corners. When it comes to remarkable workers, we spare no expense.

Ladies and gentlemen, I would now ask you to observe a moment of silence to honor the memory of a man who was in every way remarkable. I am of course referring to Mr. Marcel Duchêne.

(The Chief Executive Officer, the Division Heads and all of the guests stand up in unison to observe a minute of silence.)

More than a simple sense of decorum compels us to pay a

The Award

well-deserved tribute to Marcel Duchêne today. It is with heartfelt emotion and genuine sadness that we wish to honor the memory of this outstanding worker. Until his dying breath, his noble spirit was a fine example to all. Unfortunately, he passed away without knowing the immense satisfaction and pleasure of being decorated with the work medal.

Always ready to help and render service to his family as well as the entire community, Marcel Duchêne was a regular blood donor and a volunteer firefighter with First Aid certification.

May this brief tribute be a lesson for the malefactors and the mutineers who are attempting at this very moment to sow the vain seeds of dissension within our walls!

Marcel Duchêne's fine career as a professional grinder spanned a period of twenty-five years. All of us here know that this noble trade can prove to be one thankless job. In fact, the black particles that result from the grinding, when combined with the lubrication products, confer a blackish tint to the epidermis that proves, in the long run, to be indelible.

But Marcel Duchêne, sustained by love of his work, never concerned himself with superficial details. He understood the meaning of the word priority and he knew that bread and butter come before beauty.

There is no shame in being black of face, as long as one is pure of heart!

Revolutionary unions have made malicious insinuations, claiming that Marcel Duchêne committed suicide in an act of despair. Such insinuations are an insult to his memory.

And now we have the unique honor of presenting this vermilion medal to his wife, who is with us here today to accept the award on behalf of her late husband, along with a check for two thousand francs to cover expenses incurred by the funeral. Mr. Fabre tells me that the coffin provided by the Company is made of solid beech and lined with black silk.

(Lengthy applause.)

RESPONSE OF THE MEDAL RECIPIENT'S WIDOW

(Marcel Duchêne's widow reads from a text she wrote with the help of a social worker.)

Madam Director, on behalf of my late husband and myself, allow me to express our infinite gratitude following in the wake of Marcel's many long years of work and cooperation with this factory which is so rightly admired by all and provides for the well-being of all workers and indeed insists upon it right up until their dying hour in this factory, in this factory that you have so humbly placed under the patronage of your father whose memory is still fresh in our minds . . . Thanks a million, no, a billion, for your generous attention, Madam Director, once again thank you.

(Visible emotion on the faces of audience members, and warm applause.)

No offense, Madam Director but I would like to add that it made my husband extremely unhappy to find himself, every God-given day, with a face as gray as a common chimney sweep's. The first thing he did when he got home from work was to take several showers in a row while scrubbing his face with Saint-Michel Cologne. He used gallons of the stuff! He went through a bottle a night!

I didn't notice right away that my husband was getting darker. He'd often ask me: "Do you think I look different?" I'd always answer: "No sweetie, you still look the same." Because, you know, Marcel—Marce—was really very handsome, in his own way.

Then I finally had to admit it to myself. His complexion was turning black. It hit you like a slap in the face. But the worst thing about it was that while my husband was getting darker on the outside, he was also getting darker on the inside. He was becoming completely miserable.

Little by little, Marce lost his desire for normal everyday things. He didn't want to go out with his buddies on Saturday anymore. He was too ashamed. He didn't want to show his face in public with his face all covered in gray like one of the apartment buildings around here, not even at his mother's, and he worshipped her like she was the Virgin Mary. He didn't want to stick his nose outside the door because he was afraid someone would make fun of him. He'd say to me: "Look at that, everyone's eyeballing me like I was some circus freak." All eyes were on him wherever he went, so I'm afraid he wasn't completely off the mark.

The only times he went out were to go to the factory. It's hard to believe, but it was the only place he felt good. The rest of the time, he'd shut himself away in the kitchen, sitting with his head flat on the table, never a peep out of him. He kept so still you might have thought he was just resting, but I realize now he was already starting to die.

As for me, seeing him getting so dark, so empty and so lifeless, I started to get depressed as well. I'd get dizzy spells, mood swings, stomach pains that would shoot through my entire body. I had awful thoughts. Horrible pictures would appear when I closed my eyes. I'd see skeletons in the dark at night and I'd start shaking like a leaf. And the shakier I got, the

The Award

more agitated I got, the busier I got all day long, doing a million things around the house so I wouldn't have time to think. The more I washed, the more I scrubbed, the more I waxed, the worse he slumped into himself. A solid mass of anguish, the doctor called him. That expression always stuck with me 'cause it described his condition so perfectly.

No matter how much I tried to control myself, his depression finally got to me. I'd blow up at the drop of a hat. I was mean. I'd say to him: "Are you dead or what?" He wouldn't budge. I'd start laughing nervously. I'd say to him: "You're not gonna answer me? You want to drive me crazy?" I'd give him a good, hard shove in the back. I'd be telling myself: "Stop, will you." But I couldn't stop myself. I'd give him another shove in the back, even harder. He still didn't budge. Then I'd go nuts. I'd grab him and I'd shake him as hard as I could and I'd scream: "Move, move, goddamn it!" He was petrified, literally. I'd scream at him: "Move, move for crying out loud or I'm going to do something awful!" But he'd just slump down again, like a corpse. And so, as a last resort, I'd try to make him feel guilty. I'd say: "If your poor mother could only see you now!" But he didn't give a damn any more about his mother either, or about me, or God, or anyone or anything.

One day, I knew I'd really had it. My nerves were shot. I went to his doctor, it was Dr. Gautron who was looking after him, and I demanded a complete run down on his condition. I'm no coward, I can face the truth. I asked: "So is it serious?" Dr. Gautron, looking very pleased with himself, told me he was suffering from catatonia. Yeah, and so? Great, he'd come up with a tag but no treatment. It's often like that with doctors, all talk and no action. You guessed it, I'm not wild about doctors. I have an even lower opinion of shrinks. Other people's misery is their bread and butter. They feed off it. They stuff their faces with it. They can die of indigestion, for all I care.

As for the facial discoloration, the doctor just told me: "There's nothing I can do." He wasn't the least bit embarrassed to admit it. He just said, "There's nothing I can do," just like that, coldly, without any build up at all. The way you'd talk to an animal. And when I asked him about the way Michael Jackson's skin had been lightened, he pursed his little lips in disgust, like it was below him to even consider it, which basically told the whole story about his—about his—well, about the way he related to other human beings.

I'm not sure when it was exactly that things took a turn for the worse. I remember one day complaining to my neighbor, saying that my husband worked like a nigger. It came right off the top of my head, just like that. It was an innocent remark. As soon as my neighbor left, I saw my Marce coming towards me with a crazed look in his eyes. He grabbed my throat with his enormous hands—I thought he was going to kill me—and then he started to yell: "Say it, bitch, say it! Call me a filthy nigger. Say it if you've got the guts, go on, call me a nigger!" He ranted and raved like this for hours. He was screaming with rage. The Perezes had to pound on the wall before he finally calmed down.

There were other scenes like this. Yelling. Hitting. Fighting and making up. Highs and lows. Miserable scenes where we'd fall to the ground with our arms wrapped around each other, which, truth to tell, were our only real moments of closeness and intimacy. One night, he took me and shoved me up in front of the bathroom mirror. He grabbed my chin and jerked my face

The Award

up. "See what I look like!" he yelled. He looked at me defiantly. I lowered my eyes. But then he took me by the hair and yanked my head up violently. "I said, Look!" he said. I didn't struggle the way I'd done so many times before, just so I wouldn't have to give him an answer. We stayed like that for hours, like a couple of lunatics, staring at our two deathmasks in the mirror, until my eyes, which I'd been trying not to focus on what was in front of me, finally closed from exhaustion and pain. I finally pronounced the sentence he'd already given himself but that he wanted to hear from my lips. I spoke the words he had been waiting to hear so that the real suffering could start. The damage was now so obvious that I couldn't just keep quiet and pretend nothing was wrong any more. I couldn't keep lying to him without going nuts. I told him what he already knew. I spoke the words out loud.

Up until then, Marce had managed to keep his cool by just letting things slide, but that night he lost it. Him who'd never given a thought to what he looked like since he was a kid, probably because he knew he was handsome, all he thought about after that was the color of his skin. The color of his skin had become an obsession, a torment, a brick wall he could smash himself against time and time again until he bled. He would say to me: "You poor woman, how you can you stand living with a Black, how can you look a dirty nigger in the eye?" If I spoke nicely to him he'd say to me: "You're talking down to me, just like you were talking to a nigger." And if I happened to touch him, if I brushed him with my fingertips, he'd say: "Watch out, it stains!" Then he'd burst into tears, like a kid.

And so I began waiting for some miracle that would deliver

us both from all this darkness. And in spite of my distrust for psychiatrists, I convinced my husband to go and consult Dr. Nallet, a psychiatrist from the Medical Group here, who cured Gus's wife when she hit rock bottom. I was pretty much of the mind that you can't cure thoughts and dreams the way you'd cure a case of whooping cough. But at the same time, I couldn't stop myself from hoping because that's always been my way since the day I was born.

Sunday was his birthday. His birthday fell on All Saints' Day. I always thought it was a bad sign. I asked Dr. Nallet if he was allowed champagne, if champagne was compatible with the treatment for his nerves, one Librium morning and night, plus a Tuinol at bedtime. The psychiatrist told me there was no problem, the only contraindication with champagne was my wallet. I knew more about that than him! But I didn't hesitate for a single second. Champagne does wonders for boosting the morale, everyone knows that. I bought quality champagne, Mumm's, and I made a delicious chocolate cake out of the finest quality dark chocolate, exactly the way he liked it, that is, before he got sick . . .

After the trout almandine, I served the cake in the dishes from our good set, I poured the champagne into the glasses that my godmother gave me as a wedding present, a fabulous wedding when I think of it, two hundred guests in all, nephews, cousins, a pack of brats I'd never seen before. I remember it like it was yesterday, the giant wedding cake that everyone stood up to applaud—with a portrait of us on the top, made with pink icing—sitting on a nougat platform held up by four small white columns. It was magical. I wished my Marce a happy birthday. I said, "Happy birthday, sweetheart," and I put his birthday pre-

The Award

sent beside the dessert dish. It was a warm shirt for winter, to warm up his spirits. Marce opened the package with that painful slowness people get when they've been seriously ill for a long time. He didn't touch his cake or the champagne. He just sat there for ages, without talking or moving. He was so withdrawn it was like he was at the bottom of a pit. All of a sudden, he got up and said: "I've got some things to do in the garage." My Marce loved to spend time working in the garage. There, at least, he got to be the boss. And when I went to get him . . .

(After uttering these last words, Mrs. Duchêne begins to sob uncontrollably. The Director of Social Services escorts her back to her seat amidst embarrassed silence. The Chief Executive Officer makes a sign to Mr. Devismes, conductor of the Aubinoise Choral Society, who has been standing with his choir to the left of the stage since the beginning of the ceremony. Mr. Devismes moves to address a few words to the audience, before conducting his group.)

Ladies and gentlemen, the hymn that we are about to sing for you, "Hymn to Mr. Charles Besson," was composed in 1944 by Mr. Robert Sauzède, worker, musician and poet.

And a-one, a-two.

> In our fair and sleepy valley,
> A town sprouted overnight.
> No more do we shilly-shally,
> Yay! we say from morn 'till night.
> To us you came like a magic genie, oh!
>
> You only had to show your face,

And all hearts were won right there.
With savoir faire and wondrous grace,
You explained why life was fair.
Our kids no longer are lost in space:
Technology will give us the lead, oh!

There's more to life you did propose,
Than selflessness and being kind;
For workers to metamorphose,
We need hard work and a focused mind.
All misery we will oppose,
With love in great quantities, oh!

(The performance of this hymn is greeted by heartfelt cheers from the audience. Only the division heads and the Chief Executive Officer have not joined in the collective jubilation. They all seem preoccupied. The Director of Communication now takes the stand.)

FOURTH SPEECH

All of you have a heart. But can we set your hearts afire? The answer is: yes, yes and yes! Our Company, ladies and gentlemen, always rewards performance excellence. In order to stimulate your spirit of conformity, the Encouragement Commission, presided over by the Chief Executive Officer himself, has adopted several new measures. From now on, a list of our workers, in order of merit, will be brought to the attention of the public every month. We must, at all costs, distinguish the bad workers from the ones who are less so. The names of the last three on the list will be underlined in red. In order to highlight the triumph of the best workers, we must humiliate the mediocre. Workers, like all of us, have been provided with a soul, call it what you will, that leaves them vulnerable to shame. Let us use this to our advantage!

EXPLOIT YOURSELVES!

Ladies and gentlemen, exploit yourselves. Think only of what you have to gain. Think of yourselves first. Work yourselves to death without anyone ordering you to do so. Simply tell yourselves that you are your own foreman. That way you will spare yourselves the harassment and the annoyance of being controlled by others.

Our only desire, ladies and gentlemen, is to improve the quality of your lives. But how can one live without ever having truly existed? That is the question. How do we really know that we exist? How can we honestly verify that we are alive? Here we have, I believe, the only philosophical question of any merit whatsoever. The answer, ladies and gentlemen, has been with us all along. It's really quite simple! It's by pushing his fellow man around that a man experiences his own unique individuality, are you following me on this one, or is it going right over your heads? Let's keep it nice and simple shall we? It's when they are slaughtering one another that men feel truly alive. Because hate, ladies and gentlemen, is a wonderful propellant. It inflames. It enrages. It sweeps you away. And it injects even the most cowardly with much needed fire for combat.

HATE ONE ANOTHER!
Ladies and gentlemen, hate one another! Make enemies. It's so easy. Surpass them. Supplant them! Crush them if you have to. It isn't always necessary to destroy them. Just make them eat dust. Just so they understand! Then grab the money and run. Fortune smiles on the bold. Fiercely defend your ill-gotten gains. In this ruthless universe in which we live, our options are limited. It's eat or get eaten.

EAT OR BE EATEN
I see you cling to miserable existences. You tremble. You are terrified of life. You live your lives without being truly alive. Your work is joyless. Gentlemen, get a grip on your fears and shrug them off. Hide not in the shadows. Return to the hunt. Be like eagles. Show your talons. Proudly display your ferocity. Learn to keep perfectly still. Then swoop down on the enemy before he's had a chance to make a single move. Take him with one blow. But make it fatal.

The Award

CRANK IT UP GENTLEMEN, AND WIN!

Rev yourselves up! Speed ahead! Make those tires squeal. And you will find yourselves scaling—two rungs at a time—further and further up the ladder that leads where, where for goodness sakes? On the ladder that leads to the top, that's where. Then you will have earned the right to humiliate the next one down. The privilege of humiliating the next one down is one of man's most fundamental rights. No one here can deny this truth.

At any rate, it is not entirely inconceivable that one of you could become my successor and swing into upscale living with a microcomputer, swivel chair, the *Financial Times* on the desk and a shapely, accommodating wife, the way we all like them. Hope keeps one alive. Getting what you want, however, means you have to express yourselves. So speak up!

SPEAK UP!

Communication is our new religion. Communication is everything. It's a must. We bow down before it in worship. Join our discussion groups today. We'll talk. You and Me. Me and You. But please remain as spontaneous as possible. The presence of your supervisors must in no way intimidate you. Are you afraid of mangling our language? Are you embarrassed to be illiterate or dyslexic? Does a chimp have better writing skills than you? Nonsense, I tell you, nonsense! Tell yourselves, gentlemen, that in cases like yours, education is completely useless. I would even go so far as to say that it simply gets in the way. No one needs to be a genius to press buttons.

IGNORANCE IS POWER!

Gentlemen, express yourselves with confidence in your charming babble. With your delightful gobbledygook, propose ways of increasing energy efficiency. Our discussion groups are the very soul of reason. Our agora, you could say. Any suggestions aimed at accelerating the speed of your maneuvers will be generously rewarded. Demonstrate your imagination. Our Rewards Office hands out substantial checks to inventors of all sizes, shape or breeds.

Five topics are currently under debate in our discussion groups. Number one, must we replace our Christmas trees with plastic ones? Number two, does a moral deficit in our workers necessarily entail a budgetary deficit? Number three, is the Christian ethic compatible with receiving an income? To this crucial question I answer with a resounding yes. Number Four, how do we put an end once and for all to the scourge of laziness? By what methods can we eradicate it, once and for all? What legal recourse do we have for weeding out and punishing the lazy?

LAZINESS CORRUPTS ROOT AND BRANCH

Will we end up following the route forged by Lenin, who simply advocated isolation for the lazy? In order to effectively answer all of these questions, we need as many suggestions as possible from all of you.

Number five, how does one become a homeowner? A question that preoccupies all of you, though you dare not admit it to yourselves. Ladies and gentlemen, we know what lurks in your heart of hearts, that underneath that pretense of indifference you are in fact being consumed by a feverish desire for ownership. You

The Award

dream of buying, hiding, hoarding, then counting your possessions one by one, endlessly taking stock of your goods. Don't deny it. There's nothing to be ashamed of. All men suffer from the same vices. They guzzle and gobble, gobble and guzzle, until they explode. You might pretend to be different from us, but deep down you aspire to one thing and one thing only: a house in the suburbs with a fully equipped kitchen, living room, dining room, two bedrooms, a garage and a garden. Aspire away! Go ahead! Aspire! You have to keep your mind occupied with something, after all. Mr. Charles Besson, in his munificence, hoped that before leaving this earth, he would be able to provide each little family in his charge with its own little home. Today, the dream is within your grasp!

HOME, SWEET HOME

To help make your dream of homeownership a reality, our Company will grant you a loan under very favorable conditions. Take advantage of this offer. In thirty-five years, when all your debts have been absorbed, you will have the satisfaction of saying: this little shack is mine! Good things come to those who wait!

It is also possible for you to obtain a small plot in our Company cemetery. We still have a few tombs available at very reasonable prices. Going to visit one's own little plot is a charming excuse for a Sunday afternoon stroll. It's life's little nothings that keep families united. Does broaching the subject of your own funerals make you cringe? But you cannot spend all your time enjoying the pleasures of the here and now. Ladies and gentlemen, don't take life frivolously! Think of the future. Lack of foresight leads to terrible consequences. By taking care of this matter today, you will not be adding to the suffering of your loved ones tomorrow. Die with a clear conscience and rest in peace!

REST IN PEACE

And while we are discussing the future, we wish to remind you that a small garden contest will be held in eight months. Register now. The contest will be judged by one of our competent workers, a foreman and an engineer. An award will given for the best-kept garden. Decorate your henhouses. Hide your gardening tools, they spoil the effect. Cover your potato and zucchini patches: they aren't exactly decorative. Sweep away the broken bottles that line your plot, it creates a bad impression. Make your gardens pure poetry. Last year's happy winner sculpted his flower beds in such a way as to spell out the name of our Consortium. Become artists. You could win a weekend in Saint-Jean-de-Luz, a Sony Walkman, an electric coffeepot and much, much more. The awards ceremony will begin at 15:00 hours with the Aubinoise marching band on parade, followed by an accordion concert at 16:00 hours and the awards presentation at 18:00 hours. A buffet will be served at 19:00 hours. A fine time will be had by all!

SMALL GARDEN CONTEST JUNE 12

Ladies and gentlemen, tend your potential and make it bloom. Say I want to be the best me I can be. Fertilize your inner life. We are getting tired of repeating this, but: cultivate your own private garden. Privatize whatever can be privatized. Anything can be privatized. Start with speech. Speculate on its price. Here we have a magnificent asset and what do we make of it, I ask

The Award

you? Drivel, hot air, silly little rhymes. What a waste, I tell you! What a waste!

PRIVATIZE YOUR LIFE!

Privatize your life. What life, you ask? That is not the question! Privatize your wives and children. Wives and children make good investments. Let them mature and collect the returns. Don't let them lie fallow. That's pure waste. Draw a profit from their youthful vigor and mine their potential for gold. Exploit their resources to the maximum. The value of their labor is going up. You will obtain good dividends. Keep your investments in shape. Children must be plump but not fat. In order to increase the market value of your little family, always keep it supplied with the proper equipment. Order our latest model, the Cosmos, the crowning jewel of our collection. The Company will sell it to you on credit.

GET INVOLVED!

Get involved! Justify your motives. Staunchly defend your personal goals. You must express your individuality in every circumstance. On the production line, like anywhere else. Demand creative freedom. Creativity is everything! See how happy our artists are!

Join our team! We depend on your input. Fostering worker-management team effort is a little sideline of ours, our hope for the future. In a word: participate. Participate of your own free will in our latest scientific experiments. We are looking for volunteers. Here are the stages you will be guided through in the proposed experiment. As soon as you begin your shift, you will be injected with a narcotic. You will immediately feel yourself entering a deliciously sublunary state. Your spirit, unhinged from its normal constraints, will escape joyously on the wings of thought. You will feel free. Intelligent. One try won't make an addict out of you. You will forget your fatigue, your wife in her dirty apron and the hideous carpeting in your living room, while performing your maneuvers with the greatest of ease, as if you were under a magic spell.

Participants will be designated if none volunteer.

We will now address our foremen. Gentlemen, we ask that you use fair play with your subordinates. And please, don't be pedantic! In spite of their often revolting appearances, we must recognize that our workers are sensitive beings too. So, please, try to be courteous. Treat them gently. Toss them a kind word every once in awhile. "Hello. How is your little tyke? He had the measles? What a shame! Those overalls suit you to a T. Wherever did you get them?" I don't know. What will one compliment cost you? Nothing. And in the simple heart of the worker, a kind word is like a good kick start.

Show some finesse towards our female workers. Gaze at them tenderly. Gently murmur your orders. Be suave. Be chivalrous. Women, like dogs, are also responsive to touch.

We must be as pleasant towards our good subjects as we are harsh towards our bad ones. Bad workers have no business being here. No one can say they weren't warned! Incidents like the ones that are presently disrupting two or three of our workshops will not be tolerated in a company such as ours, where the true masters are trust and harmony. But I do not wish to elaborate any further on this matter. On this day of all days, the

The Award

solemn spirit of the occasion must not be tarnished by the pranks of a few scheming bastards. Let's call a spade a spade, shall we.

It is a man of merit that we have the honor of decorating today, a foreman like no other whose sole passion is to help the workers achieve their fullest potential on the assembly line.

Dear Mr. Pinchard, as the eldest of six children you made it your duty, from an early age, to meet the needs of your many younger siblings. With your certificate clutched in your hand, you came into our sheet metal workshop as a simple worker. But soon afterwards, your enthusiasm and team spirit earned you a promotion to the rank of foreman.

Thanks to your many talents, you have succeeded in reconciling the irreconcilable: the categorical demands of our production and the highest aspirations of our workers.

Your love of work is equal only to your hatred of parasites.

You have always remained in close contact with your men and you have succeeded in creating a warm climate of trust, equity and mutual respect. It was brought to our attention, incidentally, that a certain number of your subordinates were thinking of "doing something about the boss"—those were the words they used, I believe. Though the nature of this project remains unknown, it does allow us to underline once again your exceptional relationship with your men.

Constantly inspired by the love of progress, you cannot rest until production is flying at a frenzied pace, to the great satisfaction of our workers, who are always ready to serve the factory to which they are so deeply and devotedly attached. The production rates, if I do say so myself, are something of a hobby for you. And now you are being rightfully rewarded with this vermilion medal that we are thrilled to be presenting to you today.

(This last sentence is punctuated by a standing ovation.)

MEDAL RECIPIENT'S RESPONSE

I won't be up here for long. I'm not one for speeches. I'm a man of action.

It was no picnic when I first took over as foreman, and that's putting it mildly. My coworkers spread rumors about me. They called me a scab, a bootlicker and worse. It was jealousy that got them all yakking their heads off. And jealousy makes people mean, there's no two ways about it. Even my own children were insinuating that I was a squealer. Some words can't be taken back. And at a Tupperware party at our place, some of my wife's friends made really nasty comments about my promotion. All women are malicious gossips. All that matters to them is gab and gossip. You'd think they had nothing better to do with their time.

I'm going to take this opportunity to tell everyone here, officially, that I am not a squealer. I want to be able to hold my head high.

As far as work goes, I do what I'm told. And that's the bottom line.

Once a month, I make up a file for each worker with his name and number on it. I follow instructions. All my files are kept up to date. I put a mark on each file. I don't play favorites. Everyone gets rated on five counts. Punctuality. Attendance. Output. Behavior. Remarks. Under "Remarks," I write a few of my own observations. I weigh each word carefully. I try to be fair. But no one had better push me. I can play good cop or I can play bad cop. And if you want me to play bad cop I will.

In a special book I write down the names of union members,

saboteurs and anyone else who wants to infringe on a man's freedom to work. I can't stand shit-disturbers, if you'll pardon the expression. But there are fewer and fewer of them now. In this respect, my job has lost some of its flavor. On the one hand, I regret it. On the other hand, I don't.

In the old days, sabotage was a snap. There was nothing easier than sabotage. One well-placed kick and bam, the trolley went right off the tracks. No more assembly line! Nothing to do but twiddle your thumbs until the repair men came. It meant ten minutes less work. Parasites had it easy back them.

In this day and age, sabotage has become completely impossible, thank God. I mean, thank Technology. I'll explain what I mean for those of you who don't know. On every production line we've installed special detectors that can pick up the least little sign of trouble better than any foreman. Naturally, these controls discourage any would-be saboteurs.

But we still haven't found anything to keep a lid on the rebels. Talk about diehards. It's unbelievable. Chase one out the door and ten come in through the window. But I've got my eye on them. I never let them out of my sight. Especially when I start to sense something's in the works, a kind of excitement in the air, I don't know, something that doesn't feel quite right. I go through my usual routine, act like nothing's wrong. I do my calculations, make out my reports. Very carefully. I prepare the lists of merit, looking completely wrapped up in my work. But I don't take my eyes off them for a second. Get a move on guys, I'll say at some point. Faster guys, faster, we aren't here to nap. Move it, for Chrissake. I don't give them any breathers. Because if they get a chance to breathe, they start to think. And if they start to think,

The Award

we're screwed, there's no other word for it. I'm speaking from experience here. My job is to keep them under control. Get them before they get you. I've got my ways. I've given it a lot of thought. They get personally summoned to my booth. They show up. I let them cool their heels standing up so they stew for a nice little while. I put on my best poker-face and I don't say a word. I pretend I'm checking my forms. Very, very slowly. And then I lift my head. I look them right in the eye just to show them they don't scare me. I give them a look of complete determination. It's with the eyes that one man dominates another. And without showing the least sign of emotion, without changing my tone, with a voice cold and hard as a knife, I say to them, just like this: "If you aren't happy, the door is thataway." This makes their blood run cold. Sometimes I add: "You can go to Cuba, for all I care." Or worse, I threaten them with a report and take away their bonuses. The method is foolproof. It cools their jets instantly. And me, it cracks me up to see them thrown for a loop like that.

Because the big mouths are a lot less arrogant in my intimate little booth than in the middle of their supporters. They're a lot nicer too, there's no doubt about it. A lot more docile. Much better-natured in all respects. Like little lambs. They'd eat out of your hand.

Men in general are a lot less arrogant by themselves than in herds. I've often noticed this. Doing this job taught me a lot about human cowardice.

But often it's afterward that's the hardest. Some of them apologize. Some break down and confess when I haven't even asked them anything. Some of them suddenly become so cooperative they end up turning in buddies from their own sections. Do you think I enjoy this?! I've seen the toughest ones blubber like women. The whole thing leaves me cold. I don't give 'em anything. Consoling them is not part of my job. I'd never hear the end of it!

I'm not well liked, that's for sure. But I ask you, do you work to get liked? And to take it one step further, do you live to get liked? I mean honestly!

I don't want anyone to think my job is all bad. At the end of each month I get to reward the best workers. That's a pleasure. I hand out the envelopes, with that little something extra inside. It's a great feeling. Like my teacher Mr. Verdier used to say, virtue always has its rewards.

Contrary to what some of you might think, my job is no piece of cake. I sometimes have to deal with tragic situations that require strength and diplomacy. For example, last week one of the workers, a Turk, collapsed on the production line. Bam. Dead on the spot. A conorary, I mean a coronary. The workers come charging up to my booth, all flipped out. "Osman is dead! Osman is dead! We've got to stop production." I stop to think. I weigh the pros and the cons. On the one hand we have a dead man. On the other hand, we have production quotas. I say no. A delegate steps forward. A real hardliner. He asks me to stop production. I say no. End of story. He tries to soften me up. "Human dignity! Respect for the dead! The guys' feelings!" A whole sales pitch I know by heart. I say no. I'd rather croak than go back on a decision. I'm not the type to change my tune. When I say no, I mean no. Case closed. Dead man or no dead man, the one in charge never backs down. Especially with the workers. Always ready to kick up a fuss. Obviously, I don't win

The Award

any popularity contests with this kind of decision-making. But I'm not looking for popularity. No way do I want the workers getting chummy with me. Hi, goodbye, I keep it to a minimum. And if they're afraid of me, all the better. And if they hate me, well, I'm used to it, and when it comes down to it, I kind of prefer it that way. Oh, they keep me out of their little parties, someone's birthday, somebody's wedding, thinking they're going to get to me that way. But to tell you the truth, their little parties make me sick. You have no idea just how sick their little parties make me. I stay alone in my booth. I hear their vulgar language, the insults to the bosses, their dirty, disgusting jokes. In the middle of all the burping and laughing they drink toasts. To the health of the sucker who's paying. I'm not kidding. I let them drink. It's management orders. I haven't got a choice. But as soon as the break is over, I send them back to their posts in a shot. You have to do your job. And that's just what I do. Some of them try to buy me. Some Portuguese'll bring me a bottle of port. Some Croats offer me, what do you call their national drink again? I have no choice but to accept these gifts. But I say thanks without meaning it. Nobody buys me. My role here is to be untouchable. No more, no less. And to be untouchable, you have to keep your nose clean, no one can say any different. Too bad if I get criticized for being strict. At the beginning of my career, I was obsessed by the criticism. I couldn't sleep anymore. But with age I've become watertight. Criticism can't get to me anymore. It's the opinion of my superiors that counts. And that's it. I hope to be able to give them their money's worth right up until the end. Thank you.

(On stage, Mr. Pinchard's superiors, who have been whispering

incessantly among themselves throughout his speech, clap absentmindedly. They are visibly distracted. The Director of Communications takes the microphone once more.)

Ladies and gentlemen, our Director of Productivity, Mr. Lehrissé, will now draw you a clear and precise chart representing our car production, which, it must be said, has been thrown into jeopardy by unmotivated workers. Let us give him our full attention.

FIFTH SPEECH

Ladies, gentlemen, dear colleagues,

Competition everywhere is fierce. The Japanese are at our doorsteps. Different Groups are at each other's throats. Some hit the skids after a few lame starts. Devastated businessmen die violent deaths while their distraught wives wash down aspirins with Chivas.

We are in the midst of a worldwide economic crisis. Things are in a state of collapse. The yen is vacillating. The lira is falling. Shares in the Suez have triggered off an irreversible descent. Ladies and gentlemen, we must overcome the crisis at all costs and conduct a complete overhaul of our work methods.

Our annual production rate is somewhere in the range of one million vehicles. Our penetration into foreign markets is at a standstill. More than ever, the export market is being affected by changes in the international situation, which can greatly impede a steady volume of exports. By now, you are no doubt aware of the dirty trick the Slavs have just played on us. As for Russia, it's nothing but a heap of ruins. Our total financial decline translates into a debt of four billion francs.

The moral decline of our Firm is equally disheartening. The number of unmotivated workers, I would even say I-don't-give-a-damners, is constantly on the rise. Absenteeism is rampant. Indifference is winning.

Acts of despair have been reported. Yesterday, a man pronounced himself dead while his heart was still beating. He kept repeating: "I'm dead, I'm dead." Another refused to unload a grab. It's disconcerting. In workshop 12, a Romanian threw himself screaming onto a circular saw. Needless to say, he was killed. These spectacles are a deplorable example for our other workers, who are so much in need of inspiration. We must put an end to this now.

Ladies and gentlemen, since the incidents of despair seems to be reaching epidemic proportions, we have decided to pull out all the stops to check the spread of this disease. The strength of our nation must not be undermined by the pernicious sentiments indulged in all too often by our working classes. Our experts are categorical: despair has an extremely corrosive effect upon our highest moral principles, without which there can be no progress, no patriotism and no padrones.

In order to stave off disaster, the Director of Social Services and myself have just created a set of preventative measures which will allow us to mobilize our most formidable weapons to combat moral decay.

COMBAT DESPAIR

Combat despair. This will be our slogan from now on. We call upon you, ladies and gentlemen, to participate in this campaign. Keep a close eye on your colleagues. Listen to them. If you are alerted to any deviant behavior, notify our advisers in Industrial Psychology. You must be on the lookout for the least little warning signs. There is a long list of them. I will mention only a few: odd remarks, extravagance, profound perplexity with a tendency to procrastinate, sudden inexplicable speechlessness in the middle of discussion groups, drastic decrease in

The Award

profitability, metaphysical puzzling about destiny, questions of a highly transcendent order such as where am I? where am I going? most often employed for comic effect but which must, in these instances, be taken with complete seriousness.

The war against all those who would seek to undermine the morale of their companions by making a spectacle of themselves with acts that I would not hesitate to qualify as grotesque, egotistical and senseless, this war, my friends, will be fought without mercy. Make no mistake about it.

Though the recent wave, or dare I say, the recent craze for suicide does ever so slightly reduce the rate of unemployment, we can only condemn and punish such fatal pessimism. Pessimism, ladies and gentlemen, is a beast to be struck down and destroyed. And destroy it we will.

We are not the least bit surprised to note that these suicides, which are carried out in a noisy, exhibitionistic and highly tasteless fashion, these suicides, I say, are the quasi-exclusive trademark of solitary individuals. Solitary individuals, in the long run, always become dangerous individuals. Always keep this truth fresh in your minds.

MISERS ARE LONERS

Though we do not in any way want to insinuate ourselves into your private lives, we strongly encourage you to set up a little family to protect yourselves against nihilism, a highly contagious sickness. Certainly, we know you are instinctively predisposed to marriage. But some of you, motivated by reasons which are basely financial, still hesitate to go the distance. Gentlemen, hesitate no more! Get married! There is no shortage of women! It is a wonderful feeling to be able to unload one's heart and all the rest on a pleasing woman that is legally yours. To help you to meet your new expenses, our Consortium will grant you loans at a ridiculously low interest rate. The family, ladies and gentlemen, provides ironclad protection against the fascination with riveting images of despair to which feeble minds are prone.

But let us return to the measures we have adopted. I see you squirming with impatience.

With each failed suicide attempt, the guilty party will be subjected to a one-week layoff, followed by an irreversible transfer into a high-risk workshop.

High-risk workshops are reserved for our subcontractors. Our subcontractors welcome the underweight, the masochists, the mongoloids, the Negroid, the nervous, the nonchalant, Arabs healthy and unhealthy, reformed terrorists, pessimists (they're the worst), the obsolete, the arthritic, individuals excused from duty due to inguinal hernias or any other afflictions, et cetera.

But we hasten to reassure you concerning the fate of the aforementioned individuals. The deadly effects of the toxic substances do not appear until twenty or so years later. So there's no point in making a song and dance out of it! Besides, thanks to continual advances in modern medicine, many types of cancers, including leukemia, benefit from appropriate forms of chemotherapy.

So let's have no more squeamishness, shall we!

Backbone is what we need!

If we want to crush our foreign rivals, if we want to stop the advancing tide of their products and pulverize their records, we will have to shoot very high. And shoot we will.

Bearing this in mind, the automation of workshops five, twelve

The Award

and twenty-five has now become an absolute necessity. Let's get straight down to business, shall we gentlemen? Let's not mince words. We have always been frank with you. With workshop automation, a personnel cutback is inevitable. Two thousand workers will be thanked for their years of service. Our hands are tied, I'm afraid. This little readjustment will allow us to partially recoup some of our previous production losses. And we'll be killing two birds with one stone! While reducing our operating costs, we will also be parting ways with our black sheep.

LET'S CLEAN UP OUR ACT!
Let's clean up the company. Let's get rid of the vermin that has infested our house. We want good clean men in a good clean factory. But don't panic! The factory will acknowledge its own. We will keep only the best. Which of course means you, my friends. What's more, your load will be lightened. Your fingers will no longer cause you suffering. All you will have to do, three hundred and twenty times a day, is wait for a signal to light up on an electronic screen and press a button. Aren't you the lucky ones!

This little bit of housecleaning will benefit the entire Company. Which includes all of you who are listening to me.

To all the workers we will be thanking, we wish to say: don't look so shocked, buck up, fight the good fight, each day is a new day, the future is rich with promise, don't waste your time, time is money, profit from this holiday to broaden your mind and widen your horizons, there is no shortage of museums, art will refine you, don't take the easy road, seek out the works of higher minds, they will elevate you, for all your looking you'll find little work, win a few, lose a few, recycle yourselves, get a new lease on life, take life in hand, never lose hope, where there is life there is hope, be bold, take a chance, for example, get a little business off the ground, in a few months you will be thinking: "How lucky I was to lose my job, in the past I set my sights so low and now I have my own little business," don't regret the past, don't worry about the future, make your dreams come true, fabulous new adventures await you!

There are sure to be some idlers who will, alas, take advantage of this period of inactivity to do nothing but sprawl about shamelessly and satisfy their vices. Their agenda will consist of beer drinking and card playing. Once the party's over, they had better not come complaining around here! You sang all summer, fine by me, well now you can dance!

I now have a warning for the more gullible ones among you. These parasites will stop at nothing to elicit your compassion. Seeking only to appeal to your pity, the worst of these degenerates will disgracefully resort to begging. And so, a word of advice: be unwavering! Don't let yourself be taken for a ride! Those people only got what they deserved. Sooner or later, one pays for one's indolence.

We have thought long and hard, my friends, about the grim reality of unemployment. We are not the coldhearted monsters some make us out to be. It was evident to us that this delicate situation . . .

(Mr. Fabre, Head of Security, whispers a few words to the Director of Productivity who is standing to his left. The latter cannot contain a start of surprise.)

Those little bastards have gone too far this time! This is outra-

The Award

geous! And if they think they're going to make us crack by performing these antics, they've got another think coming! Enough's enough, godammit! Throw them out and forget about them! What are you waiting for? We aren't going to let these pathetic little shits mess with us forever!

(After this verbal U-turn that traumatizes the audience, the Director of Productivity manages to rein in his anger and let cold reason take the lead once more.)

Ladies and gentlemen, let's not lose our heads. After all, a few irresponsible wretches are not going to prevent us from doing our duty. Let the party continue!

Now, where was I? The unemployed? Oh yes. I was attempting to state that the problem of unemployment could be solved in the long run if the workers would only resign themselves to, how shall I put this, would cease procreating with such bestial persistence. We cannot help but notice that the combination of alcohol and promiscuity predisposes the workers to, shall we say, abuse the one pleasure that costs them nothing. They are rapidly proliferating. We must put an end to this kind of excess, which discredits the magnificent function of procreation in the eyes of the nation.

This is what we have arrived at. Suppose each working-class family brings only one child into the world. If this were the case, then through the natural course of marriage, death and promotions, only one child out of three would end up duplicating the, ah, the largely unenviable life-pattern of his irresponsible progenitors. We ask you to consider it. Do we have the right, my friends, to bring human beings into the world whom we know full well will later go on to become thieves, drug-dealers, assassins or one of the unemployed? For statistics are never wrong. Chronic impecuniousness leads the unemployed subject inexorably through a succession of crimes, each one more heinous than the last, until he commits the most abominable act of all, the rape of his own mother!

NON-WORKER = ROBBER = RAPIST

Needless to say, the unemployed—unemployed immigrants in particular—I'm afraid, are an extremely disagreeable fact of life for our population. People find them unpleasant. It's true. And that of course is when they don't find them downright frightening. Our politicians are aware of the situation. We have just learned that the Minister of the Interior, who has the security of our country at heart, is in the process of hiring a number of charters to fly these migrants back to the countries of their dreams. The lucky devils! Senegal! Sierra Leone! The Ivory Coast! Names that tantalize us, names that conjure up enchanting visions that shimmer before our very eyes, mother-of-pearl beaches, coconut trees, ukuleles, wild Negresses dancing to the beat of the tom-tom in Timbuktu, ah, Africa! Africa! We bid a fond farewell to our colored friends. We only hope they don't find the heat too exhausting.

As for the less pressing matter of salaries, we will get straight to the point. No bonuses. We are not in the habit of beating around the bush. If we want to remain in the race with the Japanese and German giants, we must reduce our production costs even further. Rampant absenteeism and demagogical laws concerning workday length, passed under pressure by extremists, have put a huge strain on our budget. So as not to jeopardize the recovery process that is currently underway, which will benefit all

The Award

of us in the long run, we will be forced to freeze your salaries for the time being. Ladies and gentlemen, play a role in this recovery! Accept a reduced salary! You cannot have your cake and eat it too. Show solidarity with your managers! You will derive great moral satisfaction from this. These measures, I repeat, are being adopted in the interest of all concerned! We ask you to accept them with the maturity of which you are all capable! Besides, poverty is a beneficial process, and I'm not the first one to say it. Those of you who wish to do volunteer labor are urged to step forward. We have a little surprise in store for you!

We've been told that perpetual whiners have been complaining that our salaries are ten, twenty, thirty times higher than theirs. Still the same old tune! Do not think, gentlemen, that this is due to some reprehensible oversight on our parts. Flightiness is not one of our faults. No indeed, gentlemen. It was our conscious intention to have things this way. Why? you ask. Out of nastiness? Greed? Sadism? Sheer desire to crush? No, gentlemen. It's because frustration is the strongest lever we can use for lifting the human spirit. I will repeat myself here, just to make sure that this truth fully penetrates into your gray matter: frustration is the most powerful propellant we know of for driving the human spirit into action. When a man becomes enraged by the thing he lacks, he steals it, extorts it, appropriates it. First he becomes a butcher, then president of butchers, then president period. He grows. He swells. He starts to move up. And up. And up. Till he gets to the top. Then it's glory, glory, hallelujah! He is only twenty-four years old. He has just enough time to enjoy it all before he comes crashing down to Earth. I am speaking to you, my friends, as no other boss has ever spoken to you before.

But enough said! It's a deplorable thing to become passionate about such vile pecuniary matters when there is so much more to life. The morbid resentment of some must not make us forget that there are many workers, you among them, whose powerful and irresistible sense of vocation shelters them from all forms of corruption.

It is the vocation of an exceptional woman that we are going to celebrate today, the vocation of a former tire liner who now does a bit of everything, Mrs. Josette Bourseguin.

(As the Director of Productivity descends from the from the stage, Mrs. Josette Bourseguin rises with difficulty from her seat and walks slowly forward.)

Dear Mrs. Bourseguin, it is with great pleasure that I present you with this gold medal, symbol of your tenacity and your self-sacrifice. With our sincerest congratulations.

(Applause.)

MEDAL RECIPIENT'S RESPONSE

I can see you're all in a hurry, but I just want to tell you what it was like back in '63, when I first got here all young and fresh, so the young ones know what their parents had to go through.

I started out in the mill, where they made the tire fabric. That's all gone now. They leveled it. Now there's a Mammoth store instead. It's enormous.

They stuck me over by the spool rack. That's what they called the machine where you hung the wooden bobbins to make them unwind. Me, I always had a bobbin under my left arm, and when the bobbin on the rack was finished I had to rush over as fast as I could and tie the end of its cord to the cord on the fresh bobbin I had under my arm, I don't know if you get the picture. You had to be fast on your feet, let me tell you.

And then Julien, the foreman, put me on inner lining. I guess I wasn't in his good books. Why? You tell me! Probably because I gave him too much lip. And there in tire lining I was crucified. This is no exaggeration.

The calender was the place where the cords were put through these huge rollers to make what was called cord ply. Next, the cord ply went through the cylinders, three big cylinders that could cut off your fingers in the blink of an eye. A whole bunch of them down there ended up losing their fingers in the cylinders.

So here I was on tire lining. I had this copper spike in my hands and I had to constantly make sure the cords in the ply didn't overlap one another. And when a cord snapped, I had to throw myself down on my knees so I could get under the cord ply to knot the cord back up, because the machine sure wasn't going to wait. Because of this, my knees were destroyed. I went through hell.

During all those years at the beginning, I held back my tears so much that one day I just exploded. What a scene! I was spouting tears like a fountain. I cried and cried but no matter how hard I tried, I couldn't put a lid on it. It was pouring out like Niagara Falls.

After a while, I managed to pull myself together. But I had to go under the knife. They operated on my knees. The surgeon said my meniscuses were a mess. A mess, that's what he said. Now I have steel replacements. At least they're solid! For praying, they can't be beat!

During that particular period, we had two eight-minute breaks. At first, I used them for reading. You see, I have this tremendous passion for reading. I go to the factory library at least once a month. I read anything I can get my hands on. From the worst trash to solid gold masterpieces. As long as it's a love story! I read *The Prince of Darkness* three times and there's no saying I won't read it a fourth. I'm not boasting when I say love is my speciality. I know more about love than the most experienced Don Juans. I'm not talking about that sugar coated love you read about in magazines with all those silly flutterings and complications. I for one can't stand that stuff. No, I'm talking about mad love, wild and mysterious love that sweeps you off your feet. That's the way I picture love. I'm crazy about sad love stories. I don't know how I got bitten by the reading bug. Certainly not from my parents, who can only just manage to read the newspaper.

The problem is I'm a slow reader. I'm really slow at reading.

The Award

I'll be sitting there reading and then I'll start to daydream. I'll drift off, I'll let myself go. I know what's going on. Some word captures my imagination and I'll stop and just take my time over it. Reading for me is the opposite of work. But because I read at a snail's pace, I'd only be getting to the second page before it was time to get back to the assembly line. So at the second break I'd have to start again from scratch. I'd never get anywhere. The words became a bunch of gibberish. Most of the sentences lost their punch after you'd read them twice in a row. Especially the ones about love. Because their beauty is in their uniqueness. But I could never get to the next step. I'd be left high and dry at the moment of truth. And so one day, I just gave it up.

All this is in the past now and I'm not telling you this in order to complain, but just so you young people understand the whys and wherefores of the thing. Today, the factory has changed. I don't recognize anything anymore. Everywhere you look it's electronics. Everything is controlled with buttons like in *2001: A Space Odyssey*. Progress, anyway, does have its good points.

Now we live comfortably. Thanks to my husband's overtime and the bonuses for hazardous working conditions, we were able to buy a sixty-five square meter house with all the modern conveniences. We have a real home now. Everything is different now. My husband says, so what's different? I don't know what to say to him. I guess you have to be a woman to understand.

The problem is that my two daughters keep telling me that they're never going to live here in the Town once they've grown up. There's no point in trying to discuss it. They don't want to know about it. Bottom line is, they can't stand the place. Which means that we sacrificed our lives for nothing. All that work that my husband did with his own two hands, the built-in kitchen and the two-meter-long-aquarium, I don't know if you can visualize it, two meters long, it was a heroic task, all those sacrifices, for nothing. Because my daughters keep telling me that when they're old enough to decide, they wouldn't live here in the Town even if someone paid them a million bucks. Living in the Town is like having a black eye, something to be ashamed of, that's what my daughters tell me. It's a place everyone avoids. "Live here, no way!"—that's what they tell me over and over again. Then my husband into the bargain who goes on and on about the same old thing, that we tightened our belts for nothing, that all those years of struggle and self-sacrifice were for nothing.

(In the last few minutes, members of the tribune have become noticeably agitated. The Head of Security and the Chief Executive Officer argue heatedly, while the Director of Human Resources fumbles nervously with his papers. This agitation is not lost on the crowd, which begins to show signs of concern. A peculiar noise can be heard in the room. Some of the audience leave their seats to look out the windows. With a single gesture, the Director of Productivity puts an end to their murmurs.)

Ladies and gentlemen, I ask you to give a warm round of applause for Mrs. Josette Bourseguin, who, you might say, was never short of courage.

(A few bravos can be heard. But most of the guests are so puzzled by the behavior of the managers that they forget to applaud.)

I have the honor now of welcoming Mr. François Monsaingeon, our external consultant in Social Sciences. The enlightened rec-

The Award

ommendations of Mr. Monsaingeon, whose research constitutes a considerable advance in the field of Social Sciences, will help us to better understand the aspirations of our workers, to further improve the quality of our interactions, to speedily strengthen the ties that bind us, in short, to transform our Company into a highly civilized society in its own right, a society of winners. Of course, as it is with all high-caliber scientific undertakings, some of Mr. Monsaingeon's hypotheses could be subject to controversy. Nevertheless, his worker classifications, which have now become a kind of classic in their genre, will play a key role in creating a human relations policy that will attempt to reconcile recent psychological findings with the inescapable necessity for law and order.

SIXTH SPEECH

Ladies and gentlemen,

I thank you for the honor of being invited to this beautiful ceremony. I will be presenting you with a compendium of my works in progress, which are supported by constant and scrupulously scientific observation. With the aim of demystifying an extremely complex subject, I have defined three main categories of workers: first category, the true worker, second category, the Mediterranean worker, third category, the colored and assimilated worker.

(Mr. Monsaingeon, like so many intellectuals, is totally devoid of oratorical ability. He reads his notes in a monotone, only rarely lifting his eyes towards the audience.)

First, the true worker.

The true worker is extremely punctual.

He sets himself in motion right on time.

Equipped with a wife and three children, the true worker lives in a modest abode that he usually covers with a leafy variety of wallpaper. The base of his bathroom sink is surrounded by a small nubbly carpet in some shade of green. He can most often be found in the room known as the kitchen. He doesn't want to ruin his living/dining area. The configuration created by himself and his wife, his progeny on the couch, and the television constitutes an almost perfect isosceles triangle. The chandelier in his living/dining area consists of six branches with a gold-rimmed white opaline tulip growing from the end of each. Each tulip is designed to hold a twenty-five watt light bulb. The true worker hates wasting electricity.

His dog is called Yuki.

The true worker housetrains Yuki by ramming the animal's muzzle in its own feces. Primitive as they may be, these measures are nonetheless effective. There is a lesson to be learned here. It should be noted that by dint of repeatedly sniffing their own excrement, dogs end up acquiring a taste for it. This simple principle of self-regulation, which need not be restricted to the canine population, has absolutely mind-boggling money-saving potential. I invite you to consider the possibilities with the utmost seriousness.

If one is to believe the studies carried out by Bateson and Gredys, the true worker farts more often than the other types of workers, a detestable habit that remains to this day unexplained.

Add to this his lack of financial success and we can easily understand why the true worker is no one's first choice as an erotic partner. He manages, however, to satisfy his basic needs on a regular basis, always managing to find, I daresay, a shoe that fits.

At precisely 19:00 hours, the worker's spouse fills her husband's bowl with soup, while with perfect synchronicity, the latter presses Channel Three on the remote control. If the true worker's spouse is a few minutes behind schedule, the true worker ferociously seizes the dishes and utensils laid out on the table and hurls them in the face of the offending party. Or he deals her a resounding blow with the back of his hand. Whether at home or at work, the true worker has a passion for exactitude.

The true worker is thrifty. He is committed to saving pennies.

The Award

This was the most striking of the observations published by Martel and Poron. And if the great philosopher Schopenhauer's aphorism "restraint leads to happiness" may appear erroneous to some, it is perfectly applicable where the true worker is concerned. Indeed the true worker, is content with minimal remuneration. He is satisfied with very little. For he has teeny tiny needs:

- dwelling: 2,500 francs
- apparel: 600 francs
- sustenance: 2,400 francs
- miscellaneous trifles and overindulgences (public transport, health expenses, fire insurance, etc.): 300 francs.

This brings us to a total of 5,800 francs. Out of a salary of 5,860 francs.

Remaining: 60 francs. Sixty francs multiplied by 12 equals 720 francs. 720 francs per year to put aside! That's nothing to spit at!

Therefore, we can safely conclude that an elevated salary is useless to the true worker. It could even have deleterious effects on this noble character who normally disdains excess of any kind and reduce his hourly output in the process.

Every inch a traditionalist, the true worker forbids his children to speak at the table. If the children whine, the father wallops. Concerning this point, we are pleasantly surprised to note that the true worker applies the same disciplinary principles at home that he practices every day at work. Which means that we are duly fulfilling our pedagogical mandate.

By nature faithful and affectionate, the true worker is devoid of the rebellious spirit that is so detrimental to the smooth functioning of things.

He has been celebrated on numerous occasions by our writers, our poets in particular. For he is poor. And poets love the poor. Especially, let us be frank, when they are well-built.

Completely classical in design, the true worker features two well-muscled arms fastened to a spacious thorax. Workers endowed with long arms, which permit largescale but slow movement, are classified as macrobrachialoids. Microbrachialoid designates the workers with small arms that facilitate rapid movement. Attached to the end of these arms are hands that screw, unscrew and rescrew at the supervisor's command, that haul and unload at his bidding, that crush, file or scrape to his heart's content, and that sometimes, alas, kill their supervisor when he has gone too far . . . I hasten to add that such accidents are a rare occurrence. The arms are sublimely designed bone and muscle lifting mechanisms and of crucial importance for performing the bulk of daily tasks. It would seem then, ladies and gentlemen, that by some extraordinary miracle, if you'll pardon the tautology *(at this word, a worker sitting in the last row bursts out laughing)*—excuse the tautology, it appears my enthusiasm was getting the better of me—but it would seem that the true worker was intended as nature's masterpiece of precision and marketability. It's astonishing!

All the qualities I've just listed testify to the true worker's profound and irreconcilable difference from the Mediterranean worker, who is, in a way, a caricature of the former.

(A few yawns can be detected in the audience, particularly among the workers who are occupying the last rows.)

The Award

Let us now take a look at the Mediterranean worker.

The Mediterranean worker is a migrating biped who, as his name implies, chose the area surrounding the Mediterranean basin for his domicile.

He corresponds to the worker type that is capable of great strength: prominent chest, bulging muscles, follicular overgrowth on the thorax, the pelvis (a very dense dark region indeed) and the upper limbs.

He is small or medium in size. Contrary to hearsay, our companies have a predilection for the smaller, often more rapid models. *Quo minora sunt animalia, eo majores faciunt saltus.*

But in spite of his physical qualities, the Mediterranean worker is nonchalant, even apathetic, and totally devoid of social ambition. He works without the least enthusiasm. One cannot help but wonder if he is at all motivated by love of work which, as you know, is man's unique attribute.

The Mediterranean worker is not at all pleasant.

He is dirty.

He blows his nose with his fingers.

He doesn't use paper to wipe his behind, a symptom rare enough to deserve a mention.

His erotic apparatus is large and renders him attractive to women of a certain depraved character.

Let me see, what else?

(The Social Sciences consultant seems to have lost his place in his notes. But he quickly finds it again and continues speaking.)

The Mediterranean worker is inordinately attracted to raw onions, a food which lends him a particular odor, which no one would call unpleasant of course. It takes all kinds to make a world!

He is easily led.

He submits himself to others with compliance, if not with delight. His repeated acts of provocation sometimes unleash the underlying sadism of certain foremen who succumb to their weakness in spite of themselves. Illiterate and naive, the Mediterranean worker likes to be led briskly with an iron hand. He thrives on despotism. He demands it. He courts it. He inspires it. But his spineless nature leaves him vulnerable to the influence of any prophet who happens to come along.

The Mediterranean worker sometimes complains about being unable to return to his country of birth where his vast family awaits him still. We do not believe that this is due to lack of funds as he alleges, but simply because he has found in our warm and welcoming land a spirit of camaraderie and tolerance he can no longer do without.

(The managers continue their discussion, paying no attention to the consultant's lecture.)

In contrast to the true worker, the Mediterranean worker suffers from a very marked hyperdevelopment of certain organs. In other words, he is continually harassed by the torments of the flesh and represents for you, my dear friends, an example not to be followed. Unfortunately for him, the Mediterranean worker is endowed with an enormous pudendum, which explains the nickname "melon" that he is sometimes graced with. Certain theoreticians in the field of Social Sciences have attempted to establish a link between his disproportionate genital apparatus and the subject's capacity, underused though

The Award

it may be, to generate a higher than average work impetus. I myself do not subscribe to these nebulous theories.

In conclusion, this swarthy subject presents one notable drawback: he is a squabbler and often accuses his superiors of wrongdoings both imaginary and unfounded. Nevertheless, once educated—he is easily vexed—and perfected—his resistance is unrelenting—the ensuing results, when all is said and done, are satisfactory. Furthermore, he offers the not insignificant advantage of providing the least expensive manpower in our homeland.

Does the Mediterranean worker actually have a spouse? In answer to this frequent query, I can only reply that there have been a number of reported sightings, some of which have been confirmed. I have never personally met any Mediterranean worker's spouse, but there is enough evidence to suggest I could safely wager on her existence.

According to my information, the Mediterranean worker's spouse is fat as well as ungainly. She knows and tactfully anticipates her husband's needs. Once a week, she helps him to siphon off any excess testicular buildup. This duet has three movements, which the Mediterranean worker performs in double time. For in love as in work, the Mediterranean worker is a friend of speed. If the spouse resists, the Mediterranean worker delivers a kick to the perineal region. Every country has its customs.

(The consultant in Social Sciences finally raises his eyes and the Chief Executive Officer seizes the opportunity to point discreetly at his wristwatch, signaling that he must finish his exposé as quickly as possible.)

Yes, yes, I'm getting there. I certainly do not want to bore our distinguished audience. But the range of the subject is such that a few key issues must still be addressed.

Now we come to our third category: the colored and assimilated worker.

The colored worker is completely ineducable, completely irresponsible and fundamentally selfish.

His fiduciary value borders on zero.

He resembles a turd, as much by his shape as by his color.

For him work, instead of being a never ending source of joy, is the worst of tortures, which has led us to doubt his mental health. Is he insane? Is he stupid? Who knows.

He is barely civilized.

That is all we will say on the matter, for we do not wish to risk being labeled as racists.

This system of worker classification, whose usefulness needs no further demonstration, must in future embrace a fourth category: the worker from the East, whose defining characteristics we still know little about, but which will surely require reeducation and remodeling according to true democratic principles. *(Turning first left towards the Division Heads then right towards the Chief Executive Officer.)* You have your work cut out for you, gentlemen.

(The Social Sciences consultant then looks around him and notices that the other stage members have grown extremely anxious. The Chief Executive Officer, the Director of Communications and the Director of Social Services are involved in a whispered conversation, the gravity of which escapes none of the guests. Confusion spreads through the room. We hear shouts, hurried footsteps, slamming doors. Amidst all this disorder, the Head of Security snatches up the

The Award

microphone—to the great amazement of the Social Sciences consultant, who has not finished his speech—and energetically positions himself in front of the stage.)

Dear Mr. Ateba, no one can dispute that you are in every respect a worker of the first category.

(The hubbub is such that the Head of Security is obliged to repeat his phrase. Mr. Ateba, who has not heard his name called, is summoned by his neighbors. He gets up hastily and hurries up to the stage.)

Thirty years ago, you arrived in our Consortium as a surface technician, and since then you have demonstrated time and time again your immense devotion as well as your penchant for work well done. Today we present you with this gold medal as a reward for your quiet, unassuming but nonetheless remarkable virtues.

MEDAL RECIPIENT'S RESPONSE

Thank you. Thank you so much. Thank you everyone. On this day of celebration, I . . .

SEVENTH SPEECH

(The Head of Security grabs the microphone from Mr. Ateba's hands.)

Ladies and gentlemen, I will ask you to remain calm: a third riot has just broken out in our paint workshops. The automatic spray guns were deliberately set off by extremists, Spanish for the most part. As if possessed by a life of their own, the automatic spray guns began flinging paint in all directions and not just on the cars. Our distinguished colleague, Mr. Molinier, having been urgently summoned to the scene of the drama, was sprayed from head to toe with apricot-colored paint while the villains laughed and booed. This public humiliation threw him into an extremely worrying psychological state. He is at this very moment being rushed to Saint-Louis Hospital.

Ladies and gentlemen, the situation is serious.

But Management is responding to the crisis with a cool head and a firm hand, proving to anyone still in doubt that it will not be intimidated by a pack of hoodlums.

After reading the reports by Mr. Portelli, Foreman, and Mr. Ducretet, Engineer, the Management team believes it is necessary to implement draconian measures to bring an immediate end to this fiasco. Since they give us no choice, bring out the big guns!

Number one. Anyone caught introducing explosive devices or literature into the factory will be promptly and irrevocably dismissed.

Number two. From this day forward, unnecessary wandering is forbidden, as well as loitering in front of the coffee machine or in the washrooms. The law, alas, a hundred times alas, gives us no authority to chain human beings to their stations. These days, only psychiatric hospitals have the distinct privilege of using coercion. It's an insult!

Number three. Wearing pumps has been decreed immoral.

Number four. Controversial topics are prohibited in the discussion groups. We want us all to be of the same mind. It is high time you learned about collective agreement.

Does anyone wish to object?

Number five. An expulsion committee has been set up. Extraordinary times demand extraordinary measures.

Number six. Anyone breaking these rules will be punished. The punishments will serve as an example to the mediocre. And their numbers are Legion. On the other hand, obedient workers will find themselves rewarded with Obedience Bonuses which can be immediately invested towards the purchase, on credit, of a Cosmos.

To hell with feelings!

Order is what we need!

Previous governments have served as living proof of the painful consequences of democratic latitudinarianism. We hope the present regime will undo, as promised, the mistakes of the past and reinstate the death penalty, which the entire country is clamoring for.

Our experts studied the death penalty issue. They propose that we strive to compensate for the glaring inadequacies of the penal system . We are very enthusiastic about this suggestion. We rejoice in serving our country and employing our ideas for the greater glory of the Republic. For example, each factory from the

The Award

Group could set up a specially equipped cell and place it at the disposal of the judicial authorities and their municipal officials. We're allowed to dream, aren't we?

The various methods of execution have been studied in depth by our discussion groups. We estimate that procedure 769, which was perfected in Virginia by Peter Sennett, is by far the best method. It goes as follows:

The first requirements are three pairs of rubber gloves, one square meter of cloth and a pair of scissors to make the sachet, which will house the cyanide balls.

Thirty minutes before the execution, have the prisoner don his convict's uniform and tie him securely to the gas chamber chair, which will be painted willow green. We adore willow green.

At the stroke of midnight, pull down the lever to release the cyanide balls into a bath of sulfuric acid and distilled water. After a single inhalation, the condemned man's lungs will cease to function. Death will occur fifteen minutes later. During this interval, the criminal has plenty of time to regret his crime!

But ladies and gentlemen, there are a multitude of simpler and more discreet procedures for reducing someone to nothingness. There is a large assortment of methods available to us. One only has to choose. We recommend the poverty method. Our experts have assured us this system is effective ninety-nine point nine per cent of the time.

We must specify however, for the benefit of sensitive individuals, that corporal punishment along the lines of genital torsion and other barbaric practices have been officially banned by our Company. We are not savages here.

Number seven. Surveillance will be reinforced at every level:

remote control cameras, sensors, radars, tracking devices, infrared barriers, the whole works.

(Abruptly, as if inspired by genius, the Director of Productivity scribbles a few words on a piece of paper, which he then passes to the Head of Security.)

My friends, the Director of Productivity has just made us a very interesting proposal. He suggests we block the air ducts in the painting workshops so that the rioters die of asphyxiation. We will consider this possibility in due course.

Eighth and last measure, on the advice of our Consultant in Industrial Psychology, the ban on talking we were expecting to lift will be maintained, due to the vicious use of the spoken word practiced by certain individuals.

Two inside sources have in fact reported that hooligans have been using the spoken word to insult, slander and sling mud at their superiors, and moreover to ignominiously sully the family name of our Chief Executive Officer, especially that of his father, the late Charles Besson, calling him a Nazi, a collaborator and, ladies block your ears, an asshole. We must bring an immediate end to this verbal flatulence. The atmosphere is polluted enough as it is!

I myself am an expert at verbal economy. To hell with chit–chat! Action, that's my motto! And since on this touching occasion, we are among family so to speak, I wish to confide something to you. In our home, no one gets waylaid by pointless verbal intercourse. Happiness needs no words. And believe me, no one complains about this low-fat diet. My son Jean-René has just successfully completed the entrance examination at the

The Award

National School of Administration. As for my wife, she is going to be spilling her guts, oh if she could only hear me now, I mean she is going to be pouring her soul out three times a week at her psychoanalyst's. You don't know what a psychoanalyst is, my friends? How lucky you are! A psychoanalyst is an individual who gets paid a fat salary to let people throw up, metaphorically speaking, all over him. I'm telling you the truth! You wouldn't want this job? Neither would I!

On the days that my wife is deprived of her psychoanalyst, she consults her clairvoyant, who is a great help to her, I must admit, in spite of my skepticism regarding the paranormal sciences. At the moment, her moon squaring with Virgo heightens the negative influence of Cancer, which is now Saturn conjunct, which explains her nocturnal angst and fear of spiders. However, Jupiter transiting in Aquarius is well-related to the natal Mercury and to the mid-Heaven, allowing her to realize her life's ambition in November. The next year will bring pleasant surprises: Jupiter will be in Libra!

Regarding my career, my spouse confirmed that the conjunction of the New Moon with the position of Pluto in my chart will only strengthen my reformist drive, for the greater good of all the workers.

In the meantime, we hope that the delays, which were voted in by the entire Management, delays which have been made necessary by an irresponsible few, will fortify the climate of confidence that reigns in our factory and will stimulate the workers' burgeoning vocation.

(Cries can be heard from outside. They seem to be coming from

close by. A telephone rings. The Director of Human Resources picks up the phone, listens, then hangs up. Her face has gone pale. After a brief discussion with the Chief Executive Officer, who then turns to dictate a few words to his secretary behind him, the Director of Human Resources turns to the Head of Security and relays the information to him.)

Ladies and gentlemen, a screaming riot staged by workers from six workshops has just erupted in Management headquarters and is destroying everything in its path. But our Chief Executive Officer, a longtime specialist in dealing with the most horrendous situations, has taken control of the operations. He has just sent a fax to his friend and long time accomplice, the President of the Republic himself.

I would like to take advantage of this opportunity to pay homage, on behalf of us all, to the President of the Republic whose judicious economic policy has enabled our country to make a spectacular recovery. His alliance with the Parties for Renewal has saved our country from the disaster resulting from the demagogical policy of previous governments. Let us rejoice and toast to a glorious future.

(The cries outside are getting louder and louder.)

Let us not forget that the President of the Republic and our Chief Executive Officer's fathers were united by a friendship that was as durable as it was intimate, a friendship later duplicated by their sons and sustained in a truly profitable fashion. These two remarkable men anticipated the future with amazing accuracy. As early as 1940, they extended a brotherly hand to a Germany at war, provid-

The Award

ing the latter with a thousand vehicles and more than two hundred tanks. Hence they rescued a country bled dry, our country, from a mire of stagnation and despair, and paved the way to the European collaboration heralded by Goethe and by Victor Hugo.

Let us pay homage to these noble pioneers!

The virtues they embodied, love of work, enthusiasm for the human race and faith in the ultimate triumph of Industry and Commerce, those holiest of holies, if I may be so bold, are the most splendid legacy a father could bequeath to his children. It should not be necessary to point out that Mr. Besson Junior has always made it a point of duty to follow the well-worn path of family tradition.

(The door to the right of the stage flies open admitting a secretary who rushes over, paper in hand, to the Chief Executive Officer. He rapidly scans the message, then hands it over to the Head of Security. The latter resumes his speech, but the cries coming from the hall are now so loud that he is forced to raise his voice in order to be heard.)

Ladies and gentlemen, the President of the Republic has just sent us an answer, advising us not to make a fuss over an episode he qualifies as insignificant and ridiculous. There is no use, therefore, in notifying the journalists and risk having them blow everything out of proportion as usual. The President of the Republic advises us to adopt a wait-and-see policy. And so we shall.

The miserable wretches who are acting up outside the door must in no way prevent us from celebrating the rare and wonderful event that brings us together today, the presentation of the gold medal to Mr. Serge Démaret.

My dear Mr. Démaret, our Company has reaped the benefit of your magnificent competence for thirty years now. I will not launch into a list of your multitudinous achievements, each one more fantastic than the previous. I'd never get to the end of it. I will simply limit myself to mentioning our latest model and your baby: the Cosmos, a veritable gem!

(The Head of Security is having trouble making himself heard. He begins to shout.)

The Cosmos, it was in the stars! A direct descendent of the 805, the Cosmos is equipped with a new XU 5S motor and five speed transmission which offers a compression ratio of 9.5 and a maximum torque of 13.7 mkg DIN at 3,780 revolutions per minute.

(The racket persists. Intense anxiety can be read on every face, particularly those of the guests in the first row.)

To say this model was well received by the press would be an understatement. Here are some quotes: *Libération*, "Cosmos, a Car for Our Planet;" *L'Équipe*, "Cosmos, where innovation meets tradition;" *France-Soir*, "Leopard Claws in Velvet Gloves;" *Le Parisien libéré*, "With Cosmos, Sky's the Limit" . . . Consumers have obviously been paying attention: we receive two thousand orders a day in our country alone. A record!

(Suddenly, from outside, voices begin chanting in unison :

> We want chocolate medals
> We want chocolate medals.

The expressions in the room go from anxious to puzzled.)

The Award

If this decoration comes as the crowning achievement of a thirty year career in the same company, it is, above all, your reward for being the man that you were, the man that you are.

Dear Mr. Démaret, you studied law with no enthusiasm. Your vocation was elsewhere. Then you were a militant in a revolutionary group—we were all young once—a group from which you were expelled for spending Christmas in Megève *(laughter in the room)* in the company of Miss Laforge, from Laforge & Materon Cements, who is today your spouse.

You joined our factory after those ghastly student riots. Your secret mission was to increase the happiness of the working masses who were victims of alienation from the great capital. *(Laughter)*

You were assigned to welding. But you had never touched a soldering iron in your life and proved, my good fellow, to be a very poor excuse for a semiskilled worker. *(The Head of Security pronounces this last phrase as if it were a compliment.)*

It wasn't until you began participating in our discussion groups that you showed your true colors. Your incisive mind and way with words, your innate talent for scoring the winning formula, your incessant suggestions for increasing our production norms, immediately attracted the attention of your superiors. Moving from one promotion to the next, you became what you are today, an engineer without equal, whose work is a source of pride for everyone.

(Out in the hall, the voices strike up a new chorus :

>Bang bang
>Pow pow

> Keep it up
> We'll bring them down

Nervous laughter can be heard in the audience.)

Your humanity was apparent right from the beginning. Your legendary coldness, dear Mr. Démaret is simply a smokescreen. You are a good-hearted fellow, if somewhat uncompromising. But who's complaining! You never procrasnitate . . . procrastinate. You cannot bear dialectic complexities. For you, it's either yes or no. You cut to the quick. Pointless discussions enrage you. Clarity and concision are the virtues you venerate. You are what we call a left-brainer, logical and orderly.

You elicit an unquestioning admiration from all. You always have a captive audience. You are irresistible.

You have two passions in life: cars and electronics. You are never seen without your laptop, because there isn't a single problem you don't submit to that computer. One might say your Mac knows you better than your own wife. I am joking, of course.

That indomitable energy we know so well springs from your seemingly eternal youth. As an employee, you are a cut above the rest and if I may be so bold, an employee who also managed to cut loose from the rest. For you, innovation is a matter of mere routine. You are teeming with new ideas all the time, every one of them a moneymaker.

(After an intense discussion with his colleagues and the Chief Executive Officer, the Director of Human Relations rises abruptly, walks across the room with a determined stride and exits.)

You work twelve hours a day behind your office partition. But you never complain. Work is your drug of choice. *(Sounds of a mob.)*

The Award

Which doesn't prevent you from being a man of culture. We run into you at the theater and at the movies. Sometimes without a tie! You even find the time to read!

Your understanding of public relations is at least as great as your conceptual ability. You have kept close ties with the friends of your youth, all of whom occupy positions of surprising importance. For you have never lost, my dear Mr. Démaret, that spirit of generosity that infused the ideals you embraced in your twenties. I have been given to understand that what you pay your cleaning lady is above the normal rates and that you also help her to write her letters in French. These are telltale details.

You love nature as much as you love mankind. Once your day is over, you can be found jogging in the park near your residence, in Sceaux.

The presence of so many qualities in a single being merits recognition and hence we are presenting you with this gold medal along with our sincerest congratulations. May this moment be one you will never forget.

(Suddenly the door at the end of the room flies open and a horde of workers bursts in. Terror sweeps through the audience. There is pandemonium in the first rows. Panic-stricken, the Division Heads and the Chief Executive Officer rush to join the Head of Security at the foot of the stage where they all start talking at once. Mr. Démaret, who had been heading towards the group of managers to receive his medal, interrupts their conversation and firmly states his views. Then he heads for the microphone with a determined stride. He knows that everything is on the line.)

MEDAL RECIPIENT'S RESPONSE

Ladies and gentlemen, Division Heads, Mr. Chief Executive Officer.

(The rioters who have crowded into the back of the hall start to stamp their feet and whistle, but Mr. Démaret subdues them by beginning his speech.)

We know that the fear of what tomorrow holds, the fear of—in your own simple words—simply not having enough, is oppressive, and eats away at you unrelievedly. *("My love!" exclaims a worker, amidst the commotion. "Isn't he cute!" cries another.)* The fact of the matter is we cannot bear knowing you are worried. We find it absolutely intolerable. *("Stop it, you're making me cry!" someone shouts.)* To bring an end to this pernicious dread *(laughter and whistles)*, our Chief Executive Officer, inspired by the reforms of Mr. Kichi Misayaka *("Death to the Japs!")*, once again Japan sets the example, our Chief Executive Officer thought that a lifetime appointment, yes I just said lifetime, would bring you the peace of mind you crave with all your soul, this measure being applicable, of course, to only the most meritorious workers.

LIVE TO WORK, WORK FOR LIFE
The factory and you, married for all eternity; there, I've said it. Behold, ladies and gentlemen, the joyful news which you are the first to hear. You can sleep soundly from now on. No more fears for the future! Clear skies ahead!

(The audience brings the house down. The rioters, taken aback by the announcement, consult each other in hushed tones.)

Forgive me, ladies and gentlemen, if I address myself in particular to the friends who have spontaneously joined us.

(Mr. Démaret directs his gaze towards the rioters gathered at the back of the hall, all of whom have suddenly become very attentive.)

I myself, gentlemen, had a rebellious youth. I liked Lenin. *("Queer!" calls out a rioter. Those around him admonish the heckler to be quiet.)* His portrait occupied the place of honor, over my bed. By night, I read pornographic books. By day, I shat all over capitalism. I was like a rabid dog. The working masses inspired in me some truly sublime rantings and ravings that I would then put into verse. With other adolescents like myself, I would recite hairsplitting theories that pointed an accusing finger at our teachers.

At age twenty, I wanted to approach this world of factories, which up until then had only been an image in my mind. I met sweating men, hairy men, real men. You! The real thing ripped my eyelids off. It forced me to see the truth. The frail vessel of my illusions shattered against the steel of your machines. I finally grew up.

Gentlemen, thank you! I can never thank you enough!

At your side I discovered the happiness of the real world, the infinite satisfactions of concrete reality, the masculine brotherhood of indefatigable workers. I had a head full of notions, my soul was going up in smoke; I became grounded, athletic, shackled to the harsh realities of life. Thanks to you all, I caught a

The Award

glimpse of a world that was upright, virile and musky. A man's world! And even today, when I am weary of life, I look at you, my friends, and my heart becomes serene once more.

For while these frauds, who are senile to boot, usurp the power by posing as humanitarian saints and while our country is sold off to unscrupulous adventurers, corrupt to the bone, and while shady politicians, with their shameless toadying and pompous lies, screw the country in the name of honor and patriotism, in the face of it all, you oppose these shysters who are supposed to be setting an example for the entire nation! It's fantastic!

(Applause from the entire audience)

You are strangers to greed. Your hearts remain untainted by mercenary ambition. False glory, bought titles, schemes to get ahead—ahead to what, I ask myself—none of this interests you. Ladies and gentlemen, you are the watchdogs of our moral rehabilitation—I'm not afraid to say it—the moral backbone without which a country can only fall to rack and ruin. Once again, I thank you!

(The Director of Human Relations approaches the group of rioters and invites them to sit down in the vacant seats. The rioters cause quite a stir while they take their seats. A number of them seem embarrassed.)

By sharing your humble routine existence, day after day, the inherent virtues of work were revealed to me little by little. You taught me that work is man's most wonderful invention. Work is sudorific. It's excellent for your health! *(In a loud voice.)* Work gives you dignity. *(With passion.)* *Arbeit adelt.* Work is the wellspring of peace and happiness. Work builds resistance against our ever-increasing capacity for perversion. It tames the beast and frees him from his concupiscence. It prevents the lethal boredom that assails couples after marriage. And above all, through work one avoids getting stuck fast in the sticky trap of abject sentimentality, forever aggravated by leisure and spare time, as we have frequently seen demonstrated by the professionally unemployed, poker players, and poets paid by the government. I won't mention any names.

Working conditions must be improved, you say. We are in complete agreement with you! Yes, improvements are necessary. No, more than that, they are imperative. But everything depends on how you attempt to obtain them. And if you will allow me a word of advice, gentlemen, you must put an end to the commando tactics. Do not poke any more sticks in the wheels of Progress, for nothing can avert its inevitable course. Our desires are your desires, and yet you want war? Gentlemen, get a hold of yourselves! It's idiotic to persist in repeating past mistakes.

My friends, we have entered the future. It is time to face facts. And the dawning of this new era requires, in addition to widespread technological transformation, an equally widespread transformation of mass-consciousness. We do not speak, we do not think, we do not react the way we used to. Insurrection is completely outmoded. Completely. In spite of what a few long-haired radicals might think. Look what happens to those who dare try it. Squashed! Like rats!

It's through collaboration, my friends, that we will find the way. Yes, gentlemen, collaboration, I defend the use of the word in spite of the discredit heaped upon it by History and not only do I uphold its use, I will shout it out and thus restore to it the pres-

The Award

tige that should be evident in its very etymology: working together! Working together—my friends, could there be a more exhilarating prospect! We will work together, for we need you as much as you need us. Ladies and gentlemen, let us fight for class collaboration!

My friends, we are linked together like the fingers of a hand. *(Mr. Démaret holds up his right hand.)* And so let us forget our differences. Let us embrace mutual confidence. Let us march arm in arm down the royal road of dialogue. We will create a regime of tight-knit solidarity and we will reestablish the justice for which our souls hunger.

(One of the rioters lifts his hand to speak, but Mr. Démaret, carried away by his lyrical momentum, continues his tirade.)

Ladies and gentlemen, let me tell you how proud I am of these courageous voices rising among us, prompting us to go ever deeper into dialogue and reflection. I will not allow myself to speak for my superiors, but I am certain our Division Heads and our Chief Executive Officer fully appreciate the initiative of those who, by their temerity and daring, loosen the iron yoke of routine and pull our tired old habits out from under us. Thanks to their provocation, we are revived. Without them, who would keep us on our toes? And today more than ever, we need these forces of youth, this fresh hot blood to boost us over the hurdles as we speed ahead to meet our future goals, to throw new challenges in the face of the world and to impress all our workers with the bristling intoxication, the poetry of conquest.

The events that have unfolded this afternoon are living proof that communication within our Company is not a problem and promises to take us far, very far, every day further into fresh new territory.

(The Chief Executive Officer, visibly very moved, warmly congratulates Mr. Démaret, who returns to this seat amidst a standing ovation. The former then steps up to the stage to give his speech.)

FINAL SPEECH

Ladies and gentlemen.

Our ambition spans the universe. Our penetration into foreign markets is still holding strong in spite of some weak thrusts initially. Our unsold stock is regularly liquidated in countries in need. Sixty percent on delivery, the rest payable in installments. Everyone is happy. The new republics of the East provide us with wonderfully vast dumping grounds, as does Africa. Other continents have yet to be explored.

We never lose sight of the fact that Industry, sister of Progress and Enlightenment, must extend her civilizing influence everywhere and create a community of free men all over the world.

Ever faithful to its vision, our group reaches its tentacles into the most far-flung regions of the Earth. Very soon, the project to expand our subsidiary in Nigeria will be completed. We have just set up a factory in Rio de Janeiro that will utilize more than three thousand individuals. We never hesitate to hire the locals and the labor force we assemble, for all the ignorance and scruffiness of its component parts, will nonetheless prove to be productive. For we are guided by love of mankind.

We have flung bridges in Portugal and in Yemen. Only yesterday, we received a Zairian delegation with the aim of an eventual collaboration. FSL, Poland's third leading car manufacturer, has just signed an agreement that will ensure our entry into a market of forty million souls. My friends, we will not allow these partner countries—what am I saying—these brother countries to perish. The entire honor of Europe is at stake!

On this day of joyous celebration, I cannot refrain from reflecting with emotion on what Father once confided to me, the day he named me director. With bitterness he reminded me that we were three times smaller than Volkswagen. His pride was hurt. Today, we are miles ahead of the Germans, and all this thanks to discipline and dialogue, the mother's milk of our company. Ladies and gentlemen, victory is ours! We have risen to meet our challenge! I am sure Father would have been proud to witness this triumph.

Father was not the sort of man who uses the nation's shoulders as a stepping stone, but the sort of man who devotes his entire existence to serving his country. Everything here bears the mark of his thinking, and the men who lived and worked by his side will never forget him. Time which destroys all has yet to blight the love he knew so well how to inspire.

With this sentiment of filial respect, I remain faithful to the guiding principles he instilled in me from a very young age, principles on which I have never ceased to rely since I assumed the weighty burden of assisting him and continuing his work. Working for the greater good of our nation, which in turn contributes to the greater good of the universe, such was his sublime ambition, and so it shall be ours.

Today, I would like to express my thanks to all those who share this noble ideal.

Thank you to all the work medal recipients. Thank you Mr. Donte, Miss Pizzuto, Mr. Dufrêne, Mr. Pinchard, Mrs. Bourseguin and Mr. Ateba. Your names are indissociable from factory life, from its joys and its triumphs.

Thank you to Mr. Démaret, our brilliant inventor, the peerless leader we are so very proud to have among our ranks.

The Award

Thank you all again once more for your courage and your tenacity, which have enabled a provincial company to achieve the stature of a colossus.

I wish you all an excellent evening and invite you to make your way to the reception hall where Mrs. Arjona has organized a supper, which she does every year with her usual unfailing taste.

(Enthusiastic applause from all.)

OHIO UNIVERSITY LIBRARY
Please return this book as soon as you have finished with it. In order to avoid a fine it must be returned by the latest date stamped below. All books are subject to recall after two weeks or immediately if needed for reserve.

CF